# Remember

Breelagh D'Agostino

This is a work of fiction. Names, characters, businesses, places, events, locales, and incidents are either the products of the author's imagination or used in a fictitious manner. Any resemblance to actual persons, living or dead, or actual events is purely coincidental.



*Cover image used under license from Shutterstock.com*
*Cover design by Breelagh D'Agostino*



ISBN: 9798831812442

# Anna - Interrogation Room, September 2018

"Why does life have to be so *damn* difficult sometimes?"

I take a long pause, looking down at my ink-stained fingers, then sigh. I look up at the detective.

"Ever since my brother died, I don't know how to breathe anymore. All the friends I used to have aren't there for me like they used to be, and it *hurts*. I guess they don't know what to say to me, or they're afraid to ask questions, as if *I* had something to do with my own brother's death."

The detective looks up at me with an inquisitive look on his face.

"Well, *did you*?"

I make a face that is filled with disgust, scrunching up my short, pointed nose. How could he think that? Offended by the detective's insinuation, I sit up straight, straightening my jade blouse before plopping my overlapped arms back on the table.

"*NO*! Of course not! I would've never harmed him; Drew was my best friend. That's why this has all been so difficult for me. At times it even feels like I'm struggling more than my parents. Some days I feel like I can barely get out of bed and look at myself in the mirror. Coffee helps for about half an hour. Then I eventually sink back into bed and cry for hours. Maybe I should try therapy—NO, screw that. I'm not talking to *anyone* about this, except for you, of course. I can't even let my mind remember Drew's death, or whatever anyone *really* knows about it."

It's difficult to maintain eye contact with such a strange-looking man. Detective Paisley has grayish, pale skin like a vampire, with the added bonus of his black hair being slicked back with gel. Whenever I peer into his beady little brown eyes, I get the chills.

The detective leans towards me in his seat, unveiling the stench of tuna breath. *Disgusting*.

"Please, tell me more."

I'm not ready for any of this. Just looking around this depressing room overwhelms me to my very core. The walls are a faded shade of light gray with only one exit. The walnut chairs are extremely uncomfortable, and the smell of sour milk fills the air. This is the *last* place I want to be right now. I let out a long, exaggerated exhale.

"Hhhh. I don't really wanna talk about it."

The detective pushes again, trying to get to the truth.

"It's of vital importance we get to the bottom of your brother's murder, Ms. Abston. I know this is traumatic for you, and for that, I'm sorry. Just try to think about the last time you saw Drew."

I contemplate telling the detective everything I know, trying to protect my brother's reputation as much as possible. Eventually, I come up with an excuse good enough to get out of the room and go home. In order to do this, my dormant high school acting skills must resurface. I'm going to pretend to be agitated.

"To be honest, detective, I sorta need a break from questioning today. I feel like I might explode at ANY MOMENT!"

The detective sighs, giving up on his closest lead to the truth, the sister.

"*Alright*, Ms. Abston. We'll pick this up tomorrow."

I roll my eyes before responding sarcastically.

"*Can't wait.*"

# Drew - Malcolm's Trailer, July 2017

Drew Abston, that's me. Not sure anyone else still believes that. I can't shake the feeling everyone's watching me, waiting for my downfall. As I lay here on my friend Malcolm's old coffee-stained couch in his shabby trailer, I contemplate the last few months of my life as I stare at the ceiling. The stress ball in my grip is thrust up towards the ceiling and then falls back down again into my clutches towards my freckle-filled face, over and over again. This kind of mindless activity helps me think. Adding to the discomfort of the situation, this brown and tan couch scratches behind my legs every time I move a centimeter. Malcolm is in desperate need of some new furniture.

"Everyone has been acting so strange around me lately. It's like they're walking on eggshells, and I don't know why. What can I do to make people see me for *me* again?"

Malcolm leans back so much in his recliner that his shaggy, reddish-brown hair gets poofed up in the back against the top of the chair. As Malcolm lays back comfortably, he attempts to reassure me, his "buddy." I'm not too sure we really are these days.

"Oh, come on, man. You're overthinking it. No one thinks that about you. You've gotta loosen up a bit. *And* maybe pay a little more attention to that girlfriend of yours before I swoop in and steal her, man!"

I roll my eyes. I don't believe Malcolm's weak threats for one second.

"Yeah, right, Malc. I'd like to see you try. That girl's *crazy* about me. You've got nothing on me."

I second guess myself, looking down at my tall, lanky physique. I mean, I know I've got a good-looking face, but I'm not too sure about my body. Malcolm's got some muscle on me, but hey, I think girls are into skinny guys too; Lisa must be, anyway.

Malcolm shakes his head as he licks and seals his joint.

"*Whatever*, Drew. I'm just giving you some friendly advice. Don't lose Lisa; she's the best thing you've got right now. Let's face it, hanging out with me in my trailer smoking joints and sucking down beers isn't exactly a fairytale."

I decide to shake myself out of my nonchalant state and perpetual frown, sitting up on this pungent, vintage couch.

"Yeah, you're right. I'll go call her now. Maybe she wants to hang out or something."

Malcolm cheers me on, oddly sounding happy for me. It's been a while since he's shown that sort of emotion towards me. He throws his right fist up into the air, holding his joint in between his left pointer finger and thumb.

"Way to be, man!"

As I walk out the trailer door, I make sure I'm away from any open windows so Malcolm can't hear my phone call.

I call Lisa.

Lisa picks up.

"*Drew*? Is that *you*?"

I laugh.

"Yeah, baby. Who else would it be? *Malcolm*?"

Lisa is not enthused by my sarcasm.

"Why would it be *Malcolm*? Uhh, nevermind. Drew, I wanna talk to you today. Are you free to meet up at Reggie's Diner in twenty minutes?"

All of a sudden, I feel a sense of purpose bubbling up inside of me again, being Lisa's boyfriend. Life doesn't seem so melancholy anymore.

"Sure, Lis. I'll see you then."

I walk back into the trailer.

"I'll see you later, Malc. I'm gonna go meet up with Lisa. She wants to talk about something."

Malcolm stokes the fire, something he loves to do.

"*Oo*, that doesn't sound great, man. I mean, at least she wants to see you, so I guess that's a win?"

I shake my head.

"Whatever, Malcolm. See you later."

Malcolm laughs as the smoke from his joint swirls around the room, filling it up entirely.

"Good *luck*!"

# Lisa - Interrogation Room, September 2018

"Drew hasn't been letting me in lately, and I'm *sick* of it. All I want is to have a boyfriend who actually *wants* me in his life. Why doesn't he ever want to spend time with me?"

I look down at my lap. Dark blue jeans are fresh and clean, a deep indigo color. I'm so spoiled. I don't deserve anything I've been given. Even my flawless, polished face from years of facials suffers no lack of beauty even in my darkest moment.

"Those were the last words I spoke to Malcolm before everything—"

I swallow, taking a deep breath. How am I going to get through this questioning if I have a dark secret no one can ever find out about? It would ruin my reputation.

"—before everything happened with Drew. I have everything I could ever want in life thanks to my rich parents; Drew had nothing in his final moments. How could I have become such a self-absorbed, back-stabbing girlfriend?

I just wanted him to notice me more. I was so used to the constant attention my mother and father gave me growing up. I thought I was entitled to a list of demands from my significant other—guess I was wrong. I just hope I didn't push Drew further away into darkness."

Detective Paisley wipes the sweat from his brow. I don't blame him. It's about a hundred degrees in this small, stuffy room. Or maybe that's just the guilt making me sweat through my denim jacket.

"And how would you have done that, Ms. Yantz?"

I look down at my overlapped hands that are resting peacefully on the table. The rest of me doesn't feel so relaxed; my whole body is overwhelmed with anxiety.

"Uhh, well, last July is when things with Drew started to go south. I asked him to meet me at the diner to talk..."

Drew walks through the glass front doors into Reggie's Diner, half-smiling yet obviously in a daze. He walks up to Lisa and gives her a hug.

"Hey, Lis. I'm so glad you wanted to meet up. What did you wanna talk about?"

Lisa sips her tea, then finally speaks.

"Hey, Drew. You don't look so great, although it's good to see you. Are you getting enough sleep?"

Drew shifts nervously in his booth seat, which has a large tear in it, revealing the foam from its insides.

"To be honest, Lis...not really. But I'll be fine."

Drew reaches for Lisa's hand across the table, yet she declines and pulls back.

"Drew—I know you've been getting more into drugs lately. At first, I thought it was fine seeing you occasionally do cocaine and smoke a joint with Malcolm for fun, but *heroin*? Are you freaking *kidding me*?!"

Lisa is distraught, looking down at the table as she rubs her fingers forcefully into her forehead. Despite her rage about Drew's destructive habits, she still cares about her boyfriend.

"And what have you been doing for work? Why do I never *see* you anymore, baby?"

Lisa now decides to reach for Drew's hand for comfort. He reaches back, the two of them playing with each other's fingers as they sort through their relationship crisis.

"Don't worry, babe. I've been working with my dad at his landscaping office, helping him with the books. You know how good I am with numbers, *right*?"

Lisa sniffs as she tries to fight back her tears.

"You *are* good with numbers."

Drew smiles at his girlfriend, trying to reassure her.

"Everything's gonna be fine, Lis. I'll quit, for you. Besides, I can't think straight anyway. I don't wanna *lose* you, Lisa. You're my everything."

Drew slides over to Lisa's booth, putting his arm around her.

"We'll make it through this rough patch, I promise. I wanna be the kinda man who can support you. Remember how we talked about getting married back in high school?"

Lisa starts to laugh.

"Yeah, we were freaking *idiots* back then, Drew. But I still see a future with you, as long as you can get it together."

Drew looks deeply into Lisa's eyes before kissing her on the lips.

"I will, Lisa. For us."

Back in the interrogation room. Is this *really* my life now? Man, I miss Andrew so damn much.

"So then what happened, Lisa?"

I look up at the clock. Time to get back to work at the bowling alley. Work is always a great excuse to get out of questioning.

"I—I think I'm done for the day, Detective Paisley. Work's calling my name."

"Alright, Ms. Yantz. Thank you for your time. Hopefully, we can continue this soon."

# Malcolm - Interrogation Room, September 2018

"My buddy Drew acts so strange whenever he's with his girl, Lisa. I think Lisa is getting annoyed that Drew isn't fully committed to their relationship. I tried telling him a few times, but he won't listen. Maybe he'll listen if my Uncle Ted shows up at his trailer. That oughta teach him a lesson."

Detective Paisley sighs as he reads out of my raggedy composition notebook.

"Hhh. This isn't looking good for you, Malcolm. *Threatening* your best friend? You could get in serious trouble for this now that he's dead."

I gulp down the tennis ball of regret that's been forming at the top of my esophagus.

"What can I say that won't make me look guilty, detective? I'm a writer. I can't help myself. Sure, it was dumb as *hell* to write all that down—I'm a freakin' idiot."

The detective flashes his judgy eyes at me once again.

"Well, only time will tell, Malcolm. As long as your stories about Drew line up and we figure out who the killer is, you're off the hook. For now, you need to tell me everything you know about Drew Abston. You two dealt together, *didn't you*?"

I can't believe I'm gonna get busted for this. Nobody better come after me. Otherwise, they'll have my fifty cal to go through first. Before responding to the detective, I take a moment to think as I lay back in my seat, lowering my head to my baggy, worn-out jeans and camel-colored, dirty work boots.

"Yes, detective. Drew and I started dealing out of my trailer sometime in the spring of twenty-seventeen. At first, it was just weed, then it turned into cocaine, and then heroin sometime in July. Drew and I would smoke joints together *all* the time; we'd even entertain a little coke now and then to amp things up. Then one day, Drew wanted to 'sample' our heroin supply to see what he was missing out on. Personally, I would never touch the stuff."

Detective Paisley asks a question with an obvious response. Although, I'm a moron, so maybe the answer isn't *that* obvious.

"And why is that?"

I tap three fingers on the table in my laid-back, relaxed position. I then move forward in my seat towards Paisley, intertwining my fingers to show that I'm dead serious. Ah, that was the wrong choice of words.

"Just because I push it doesn't mean I need to ruin my *own* life over it. I don't know what the guy was lookin' for, detective. Drew was always a mystery. You never knew what mood you were gonna get from the guy. He was very impulsive, always making rash decisions fueled by emotion."

"Tell me more about that, Mr. Savona."

I proudly think back on the good ole days with Drew.

"Well, things *really* started heating up with our business in early December of twenty-seventeen...."

It's late in the afternoon, and Malcolm Savona is busy at work in his trailer, equally separating supplies into Drew's half and his half. A cigarette dangles from his mouth as he works, reggae music softly playing in the background. Drew comes stumbling into Malcolm's trailer, high as a kite. He has bags under his eyes, and his skin color is pale, yet more like yellow snow. Malcolm confronts Drew's erratic behavior, as if he's the poster child for rationalism in America.

"*DREW*—get your act together, man! Here, take your half. You've gotta sell it all by the end of the month, or else we might be visited by the *drug fairies*. Do you think you can do that?"

Drew looks Malcolm straight in the eyes, about three inches away from his face, his breath reeking like a sour onion.

"Man, I know what you did, Malcolm! You and Lisa, *cheating*, behind my back?! I thought you and I were bros, Malc! And Lisa... ah, Lisa. We were supposed to get married—I'm DONE with her."

Malcolm takes a step back, holding up his hands.

"Woah, woah, woah—let's just set the record straight. She didn't *cheat* on you, man. I take full responsibility because *I* kissed *her*. Don't take this out on Lis."

Drew stumbles again.

"You don't get to call her that, Malcolm! She's my—she was *my* girlfriend for almost *six years*! I HATE YOU—you ruined my life!"

Drew charges into Malcolm, Malcolm crashing into the lamp behind him. Drew throws a punch at Malcolm's face, but he's too weak from the drugs to make much of an impact. Malcolm throws Drew up against the wall in his trailer, almost crushing his cuckoo clock.

"I didn't ruin your life, Drew! *You* ruined it. I don't wanna see you like this, man. You need *SERIOUS* HELP!"

Drew sinks down onto the cold, linoleum floor in Malcolm's kitchen, bursting into tears.

"I just want my life back, Malcolm, before—"

Drew looks around the room, gesturing at the table full of drug baggies.

"—before all of *THIS*!"

Malcolm rolls up his sleeves and gets back to work.

"I don't know what to tell you, Drew. You said you wanted in on this business, so now you have to play your part, at least until all of our product is gone."

Malcolm hands Drew his duffle bag filled with product.

"You up for this?"

Drew wipes the tears from his face and gets back up.

"Sure, *whatever*, Malc. I'm outta here."

I sit back up in my seat after telling my story to the detective.

"And that's the last I ever saw of Drew Abston, I *swear*."

Detective Paisley looks satisfied.

"Very good, Malcolm. Thank you for your honesty. I'll call you if I have any more questions."

We shake hands, and I'm free to leave, hopefully for good.

# Rebecca - Interrogation Room, September 2018

"I was always worried *sick* about my kids. They needed to listen to me, but they just *wouldn't*, especially Drew. I knew Drew was into something shady; I tried confronting him about it several times. He would always brush it off as 'none of my business' or tell me not to worry. Anna was another story—that girl was constantly consumed by her brother's drama ever since they were young. I kept telling her she needed to focus on her own future and not risk losing her dream job at the magazine over Drew's problems. Sadly, she didn't listen to me, and it was the biggest wake-up call of her life."

Detective Robert Paisley jots down a few phrases on his notepad, making a face that requires police training to decrypt.

"And where is Anna working now?"

I stomach a sip of coffee from my styrofoam cup and think about the hopes and dreams my Anna is still clinging onto for dear life.

"Anna is working on her own blog right now as she searches for another job as a freelance writer. For money, she's been working as a dog walker."

Detective Paisley takes a sip of his own styrofoam coffee, not seeming to mind the taste.

"That's good to hear, Mrs. Abston. And your husband, how is he dealing with the loss of your son?"

I shift uncomfortably in my seat, fighting back the tears.

"Oh, Roger? His demeanor has changed, absolutely. He's not how he used to be, before...."

I can't fight back the tears any longer.

"...before our Drew di—was brutally *MURDERED*!"

Agitation is coursing through my veins, leading me to dig my fingers into my curly brown hair as I lean forward with my elbows on the table in front of me.

"Drew's body was left out in that field, alone...nobody was there to mourn him! And he was gone with just *ONE* BULLET TO THE HEAD?!"

I'm standing now, on the edge of a mental breakdown.

"IT DOESN'T MAKE ANY SENSE!"

I take a deep breath, trying to regain my composure before I get arrested.

"Why can't you find my son's killer, detective?! And you want to question *me*?! I can't do this anymore!"

Detective Paisley tries to cool me down with his words and by patting the air in front of him with both hands.

"Woah, *woah*, Mrs. Abston. *Please*, calm down. We're done for the day. I'll call you if I have any more questions. Your husband will be coming in to speak to me tomorrow, so I'm sure he could fill me in for the time being."

My body is trembling as I stand in the corner of the interrogation room, yet somehow I'm able to get my legs moving.

"Okay, detective. Thank you for understanding."

Detective Paisley stands up, knowing better than to shake my hand in a situation like this. He motions his hand up for a quick wave goodbye.

"Have a good night, ma'am."

"You too, detective."

I am *OUT* of here. It's going to have to take some huge revelation in Drew's case for me to *ever* come back here again.

# Roger - Interrogation Room, September 2018

"Daddio, they used to call me, when they were young, of course. Anna and Drew, inseparable siblings from the start. It's no wonder Anna insisted on worrying her life away over Drew's problems. I raised my kids better than that; I told them to never stop pursuing their dreams. At least they always had caring hearts, but at what cost? Caring didn't exactly end so well for either of them this past summer. There is only so much care you can give someone who doesn't want to receive it. Ultimately, everyone has to make their own decisions and face the consequences of life. I don't know what else I could've done."

Detective Paisley is slouched over, jotting down a few phrases on his legal pad, psychoanalyzing me in the process. I don't appreciate that. He clears his throat and looks up at me.

"That seems a little *harsh*, don't you think, Mr. Abston?"

I sit up straight, adjusting my powder-blue button-down shirt.

"Maybe to some, but I don't accept second best from my kids. It's not like I would *punish* them for not doing their best. It was more of a subtle understanding we had. I wouldn't congratulate them on any victory or achievement unless it was number one. Maybe it was rigid parenting, but they always knew how much I loved them at the end of the day."

Detective Paisley sits up.

"Are you *sure* about that, Roger? Because it seems to me that Anna and Drew were really struggling last month based on the stories I've been told."

Anger starts boiling up within me like molten lava, yet I force it down so as to not act unprofessionally.

"I don't like this insinuation you have that I'm a *bad* parent, detective. What are you getting at?"

The detective reaches for more answers with another question.

"You said Drew did accounting for your landscaping company, correct?"

My hands are now interlocked on the table as I answer the detective's meaningless questions.

"Yes, from time to time, Drew would help out at the main office. He used to be there more often right after graduating high school. That only lasted about a year before he got sick of me and wanted to do his own thing."

Detective Robert Paisley continues with his line of questioning.

"What did he do for work after leaving your company?"

My recollection of Drew's life isn't too shabby. I think I can remember.

"Let's see...Drew worked odd jobs here and there as a cashier for Frederick's Supermarket, a busboy at Reggie's Diner, a house painter, he plowed driveways in the winter, and at one point, he entertained landscaping a few houses for me."

Paisley records more information on his pad of yellow paper.

"And what about his most recent line of work, *dealing*?"

I clear my throat, not because anything is there, but because I'm starting to feel very uncomfortable.

"I would never condone an occupation such as that, detective, if that's what you're asking."

Paisley looks straight into my soul, responding with an attitude.

"I never said you would."

My eyes become wider as I press my lips together and look at and respond to the detective, sick of his interrogation.

"Okay, I just wanted to make that *crystal* clear for you."

The detective cuts straight to the chase. He doesn't appreciate my tone, although I don't appreciate his either.

"Do you think your son was killed by the cartel?"

I'm taken aback.

"To be honest, detective, I think that is *very* possible. I know Drew was using, so maybe he dipped into his supply and owed them some money. You never know with those types of people; there isn't an *ounce* of good in those money-hungry snakes."

It seems like that was enough to get the monkey off my back, as if *I'm* the reason Drew is dead.

"Thank you, Mr. Abston. I'll get back to you if I need more; your time today proved to be very useful."

"Glad I could help."

We shake hands, and I take off.

# Rick - Interrogation Room, September 2018

"Ever since AP Chemistry junior year of high school, I knew Drew was a special case. He was fun to talk to and hang out with, but at the end of the day, he would always drag you down with his drama. We had been friends since the sixth grade, but he started to change junior year. We weren't hanging out as much as we used to. A lot of it having to do with our rivalry over Isabel. That's why we hadn't spoken in years since graduation. And in late December of twenty-seventeen, before Drew bolted and completely disappeared, I was looking to reconnect with him. Both twenty-two year olds at the time, I knew Drew always had an entrepreneurial spirit, which is why I thought we'd make good business partners. And maybe we could've been friends again, for *real*."

Detective Paisley looks straight into my eyes, possibly looking into my soul? It's creepy.

"Tell me, Rick, what happened when you tried to reconnect with Andrew?"

Memories begin to unfold in my mind as I sit up in my seat, putting both hands into the pockets of my jeans.

"Well, I was on the way to see a movie with my friend Isabel right before Christmas, when all of a sudden we ran into Drew...."

Rick and Isabel are walking down the streets of Woodbank, passing a convenience store. Out of nowhere, they see Drew standing outside, leaning up against the exterior wall of the store with one foot.

Rick greets his friend, whom he hasn't spoken to in years. He reaches for a handshake, which Drew hesitantly gives him.

"Drew—is that *you*? It's great to see you, buddy! I've been wanting to talk to you. How've you been?"

Drew gazes at his long-lost friends.

"It's great to see you too, Rick. It's been a while. And Isabel, it's been *way* too long since I've seen you."

Isabel reaches in for a hug.

"I'm so happy to see you, Drew. I'm sorry I haven't kept in touch since high school."

Drew wipes his hand across his face, which is flushed and filled with acne. He can't seem to stop scratching his arms and face.

"I *know,* Izzy. I'm sorry too. I was so caught up with Lisa and, honestly, my own crap. I should've been better friends to both of you."

Rick nudges Drew's arm.

"Ah, don't worry about it, man. We have plenty of time to make up for it now. How about we meet up for coffee later at Reggie's? I wanna talk to you about a business proposition; I think you'd be pretty interested."

Drew takes a sip of his ginger ale.

"Alright, Ricky. I think I could do that. You buyin' me a coffee, though? Cause I'm not coming unless you are."

Rick laughs.

"Yeah, sure, Drew. I think I could manage that."

Drew tries standing up straight, struggling to keep his balance. Isabel reaches for his arm.

"*Are you okay*, Drew? You don't look so great."

Rick and Isabel take a step closer, noticing that Drew's eyes are glazed over. He looks up and smiles at Isabel.

"I'll be alright, don't you worry about me, beautiful."

Isabel can't help but blush when her short-term high school boyfriend just brought back all sorts of feelings. Meanwhile, Drew is fading, almost falling asleep in the middle of town as judging eyes pass by. Rick reaches his arm out to help Drew stand up.

"*Drew*? What's up, man? Are you using?"

Rick props Drew up against the brick wall next to the convenience store. Drew responds with a half-asleep answer.

"Me? Using *what*? My *brain power* to fight crime?"

Drew exhales a long, goofy laugh as he karate chops his hands through the air.

"*Of course.*"

Rick and Isabel exchange a concerned look, both noticing the track marks on Drew's arms. Isabel grabs Drew's hand, then starts dialing the number of a substance abuse hotline.

"Don't worry, Drew. We're gonna get you the help you need."

My story is cut short due to the detective's lack of patience.

"And you got Drew the help he needed?"

I look down at my lap.

"I really wish we did. Drew never met up with me at the diner that night for, well, obvious reasons. The next day, Isabel and I went to Drew's trailer to check on him, but he was already gone. He left everything behind him, even his gecko, Marty."

Detective Paisley looks up from his notepad.

"Why do you think he left?"

"I really don't know, detective. Maybe he owed money to someone?"

Detective Paisley exhales loudly, seeming disappointed with the information I provided him.

"That seems to be the running theme. We'll look into it further."

The detective gestures his hand towards the door.

"Thank you, Mr. Malloy. You can go now; you have a nice day."

I half-smile, not really feeling like I helped much.

"You too, detective."

# Isabel - Interrogation Room, September 2018

"I had a crush on Drew since the eighth grade. Why I never did anything about it all those years, I don't really know."

I shift slightly in my seat, fiddling with the seam on the right side of my sky blue jeans.

"I also had a crush on Rick since the seventh grade. I didn't end up dating either of them during middle or early high school. Perhaps I was too caught up in the fantasy of which one I would be with. Two love tales, being told in their own way, neither better than the other. Who would I pick if they both said they liked me? That was always the predicament I had in my mind. Whereas in reality, neither of them ever made it clear if they liked me or not. Both were sweet and friendly to me throughout our years of being friends, although Rick *definitely* made more of an effort to be my friend."

Detective Paisley seems intrigued; he must be a romantic.

"Why could you never decide between your two crushes, Isabel?"

I shrug my shoulders, then fixate my fingers on the paper cup of water in front of me.

"I was indecisive, I guess, and also shy, which is why I never told them how I felt. And then, out of nowhere, Drew told me he had feelings for me junior year of high school, which *completely* threw me for a loop. We dated for a week, which was *amazing*, until he decided he liked Lisa more than me; that *really* hurt. But look how things turned out with Rick and me."

I smile as I think about my kind, thoughtful boyfriend.

"At least we got our happy ending, although I sometimes wonder what could have been between Andrew and me if I had only told him how I felt years ago. Maybe if we had dated sooner, I could've been a better influence on him than Lisa Yantz. Lisa can be sweet when she wants to be, but let's face it, that woman has *always* loved trouble. It's no wonder she ended up cheating on Drew with Malcolm;

Malcolm—the *real* reason this all happened. I think it's fair to say he ruined Drew's life."

Paisley gets ready to jot down some more notes.

"Why do you think that, Ms. Tabbert?"

Thinking about Malcolm Savona always gets me fired up; I do *not* like that guy. Never have, and never will.

"Are you *kidding me*? That *dope dealer*? He for *sure* got Drew into dealing and doing drugs. He may not admit it with his 'holier than thou' attitude, but he *did* it."

Detective Paisley leans in towards me, curious now more than ever.

"Did *what*, exactly, Isabel?"

I've got my theories; not sure if they're true or not, but I've got them. That's what happens when your best friend dies; you're constantly thinking about who may have done it, how, and *why*.

"Well, I'm not too sure if he killed Drew or not; anything is possible at this point, as I'm sure you know, Detective Paisley. But in a sense, I think he *did* kill Drew Abston just by being his friend, if he was even that."

The detective scribbles a few words on his notepad, then looks up at me. He doesn't seem too convinced that Malcolm is Drew's murderer, unless that's just his poker face.

"Ms. Tabbert, thank you for your time today. I'll look into these claims further. You were very helpful in our efforts to find Drew's killer and bring justice to his family."

He reaches out to shake my small, dainty hand with a firm grip and sandpaper touch.

"You have a good day now."

I zip up my bomber jacket.

"Thank you, Detective Paisley. You have a nice day also."

# Gene - Interrogation Room, September 2018

"I've known the Abstons for years, ever since they moved in next door during the summer of two thousand and seven. Me being an old crank, we never chatted much. That Drew kid always seemed like trouble. Anna was always a sweetheart, following her older brother around like he was the leader of their duo. If you ask me, there was never anything impressive about the Abston boy. I would've rather have seen a more mature, responsible man come out of that household, but here we are. I'm going to make a better effort to get to know that family. I want to help in any way I can. I know what they're going through is rough, and I want to be a good guy for once in my life."

Detective Robert Paisley digs for specifics.

"How well did you know the Abstons before Drew died, Mr. Henry? And how often would you say you talked to them?"

This flannel is getting hot, so I fan it on and off my abdomen a few times before answering.

"Well, I kept to myself most of the time in those days. By 'days,' I really mean 'years.' Occasionally, I would see Rebecca or Roger outside in the driveway, and we would wave to each other. Sometimes we would even exchange a wheelbarrow or a few gardening tools; that was about it."

The detective clicks his pen in and out, over and over again, before finally hitting me with his next question; such an *annoying* habit.

"Did you ever interact with Anna or Drew over the years?"

My mind goes back to the darkness of Drew's early life.

"I spoke to their son a few times, regretfully. Drew Abston was always a troubled boy; I knew it from the start. When Drew was around twelve or thirteen years old, I saw him drown a frog in my pool. He looked up as soon as the deed was done and told me, 'I took care of it, Mr. Henry,' as he stared back at me with his wide, devious, close-lipped smile. That was the day I knew to stay away from him—and I told everyone in the neighborhood to do the same. What kind of neighbor would I be if I didn't?"

Detective Paisley seems to take offense to my judgment of Drew in his early days; he's starting to get worked up.

"And I suppose you thought that was noble, to warn everyone about a *child* who took the life of a *small* creature in your neighborhood?!"

I'm at a loss for words, so I stumble on whatever I have left in my mind.

"Well, yes...*but—*!"

Detective Paisley pushes the issue further.

"And what about *Anna*, Mr. Henry? Did you ever interact with *her* throughout your years of being neighbors?"

Oh, sweet Anna, always getting caught up in her brother's issues. I gulp from the pressure of being interrogated before elaborating for the detective.

"All I know about Anna is that she came to my house a few times to sell cookies for her troop. She would wear the biggest smile on her face and was always so polite. It's a shame she would stick up for her brother every time he got into a fight at school. Anna was just a *kid*, much more than

Drew was when they first moved in next to me. I would hear about *all* of the drama from their mother, Rebecca. She's the one Abston I couldn't keep at a distance."

Detective Paisley lets out a long, exhausted sigh; he seems displeased with my responses.

"So, earlier, you said you *rarely* spoke to the Abstons, yet now you're telling me that you and Rebecca Abston spoke *regularly*?"

The detective abruptly stands up, propping his fists onto the table as he leans in only an inch from my face.

"WHICH IS IT, *GENE*?!"

I panic, darting my eyes all around the room as I inhale and exhale a few short breaths.

"Okay, OKAY! I may have stretched the truth about not being close with their mother—I'm sorry about that, detective...really, I am. I just thought if I sounded like her best friend, you would think *I* took the poor boy's life to get justice for Rebecca and her miserable family. Do you know how tragic it was for them to hear their boy was a *heroin addict* and a *drug dealer*? And then to have to deal with the fact that he was *missing* for months?! That boy *TORTURED* HIS FAMILY!"

I burst into tears for the first time since my wife died thirteen years ago. As I'm crying, I notice the detective release his fists from the table top and sit down; he seems to have calmed down.

"Now *that's* the kind of raw emotion I was looking for, Gene. Don't worry. You're not in trouble, at least not yet. We still haven't found Drew's killer, so everyone's a suspect at this point."

The sadistic detective reaches out to shake my hand.

"You have a good night now, Mr. Henry."

I can't believe what I'm seeing unfold in front of me; how a man could be so ruthless towards an old guy like myself. I thought my kind were to be respected; guess that's a solid gold lie. I reach to shake Detective Paisley's hand.

"You too, sir. You too."

# Drew - In his trailer, December 2017

I'm finally sleeping peacefully on this lumpy mattress, getting some solid rest for once, knowing my true friends are there for me. Maybe I'll *actually* go to rehab starting tomorrow. Interrupting my dreams is a loud kicking in of the door, which wakes me up abruptly. I quickly turn on the lamp next to my bed to see who's in my trailer.

Enters Ted, Malcolm's uncle, who's carrying a shotgun in one hand as he forcefully approaches my bedroom. The shotgun barrel now rests on the side of my head.

"Wakey, wakey lil' boy. Ha ha! I *said*, IT'S TIME TO GET UP!"

Ted rips my covers right off and picks me up by the collar of my t-shirt. I'm in a daze.

"Wha-what is this, Ted? *Why* are you in my trailer in the middle of the night?!"

Ted slams my back up against the wall in my bedroom, positioning the shotgun against my head again.

"You better listen here, lil' boy. My nephew Malcolm's not gonna put up with your BS anymore, and neither is that cute little cartel you two are workin' for. I know you went through your whole supply, DREW! You better think QUICK—before someone *much* more dangerous comes after you AND Malcolm! I'm sick of this. You lil' punk thinkin' you can handle your shit! You're a junkie—and that's all you'll ever be if you don't get it together! I better see you work your ass off to get sober and then find a way to get that money back for the cartel, Drew, or else little Ginnie and I won't be so forgiving next time we show up at your place in the middle of the night!"

He tosses me back down to the ground before storming out of my trailer. I'm left lying on the floor, feeling pathetic and completely terrified. I lay there for about ten minutes with my face against the stale, red carpet, shaking from withdrawals and fear.

Finally, I get my act together and get up, wiping the tears from my face. No high is worth losing my life over; I've gotta get out of here. I zip up my jacket, quickly grab my wallet, keys, and phone, then pack a few clothes in a duffel bag before taking off in my old eighty-five station wagon.

I drive for about a hundred and fifty miles, only stopping for gas and cigarettes before reaching a farm somewhere in New Hampshire. I pull my squeaky car up to the property next to an empty barn, where I decide to spend the night on a bale of hay. As I lay down on this scratchy straw in the pitch-black hayloft, I contemplate my next move; I can't *seriously* go back to Woodbank. Ted and Malcolm are there looking for vengeance. Even worse, the *cartel* knows I'm there.

My mind races for nearly an hour before I finally start to doze off at four-thirty in the morning. Right when I'm about to fall into a deep sleep, I'm awakened by the sound of the barn door opening and closing abruptly. My skin crawls as my life is once again in danger; I don't dare move a muscle.

I hear someone climbing up the ladder to the hayloft. *Who could possibly know I'm here*?! I frantically look around for a weapon to defend myself with; too bad I don't have a gun. Noticing a horseshoe on the ground, I quickly equip it in my right hand as I patiently wait for the stranger to climb to the top of the ladder. Halfway up, he yells out to me, providing a warning.

"WHO'S UP THERE?! I saw your car parked outside my barn; we don't accept freeloaders here. You have about *three* seconds to drop whatever weapon you're holding before I shoot you. ONE...TWO..."

Completely overtaken by fear, I drop the horseshoe, which makes a thunk as it hits the shabby wooden floor. This lets the stranger know I have surrendered entirely. The man comes to the top of the ladder, reaching the hayloft I'm occupying.

"...*THREE*!"

The old man points his revolver at my head, causing me to put my hands up.

"I'm sorry—*I'M SORRY*! I just needed someplace to stay tonight! You don't know what kind of trouble I'm in, sir. If you could just let me stay here tonight, I'll be out of your hair by tomorrow—I *promise*."

The owner of the barn questions me while aiming his revolver at my head.

"What kind of trouble you in, son?"

My back is up against a bale of hay on the ground with my legs bent in towards the rest of my body as I succumb to the will of this stranger.

"I deal heroin, and I'm an addict. I went through my *whole* supply, the supply I was supposed to sell within the month. Now I'm screwed. My buddy's uncle just threatened to kill me, and I have a feeling Malcolm's not too far from the same threats. They both own guns and are *pissed* at me; I don't blame them—I'm a junkie. And now the cartel could come after me too if I don't pay what I owe them! COULD YOU *PLEASE* HELP ME, SIR?!"

I reach out and grab the man's feet, bowing down before him, begging for mercy as I weep on top of his boots. This is my *all-time* lowest moment.

The burly old man tucks his gun away behind his back, reaching his hand out to pick me up.

"Son, you need all *sorts* of help, and I might be able to give that to you."

I look up at the man, sucking up my snot as I mop up these tears with my sleeve.

"*Really*? You would do that for me, sir?"

"Yes, of course, son. But you're gonna have to do your fair share of work around here if you're gonna be staying with us a while. First, we're gonna put you in a rehab facility. Then, after two weeks, you'll be full-time on the farm, lifting bales of hay and feeding the goats; doing whatever I say, in other words."

I'm not too keen on rehab, but I don't have any other choice. I can't keep wasting my life away.

"Of course, sir. I'll do anything."

The man introduces himself.

"Call me Curtis. My wife, Samantha, and I are gonna get you well, son; don't you worry."

I dive in to hug Curtis, my savior.

"*Thank you*, Curtis. You don't know how much this means to me. You're saving my life."

"*Ooph*! Of course, son. And what's your name?"

I stand up to shake Curtis' hand a little too enthusiastically.

"I'm Drew, Drew Abston."

"And where are you from, Drew Abston?"

Thinking back on all the memories of Woodbank, good and bad, I answer the man as I wiggle my fingers around in my front jean pockets.

"A town called Woodbank in Massachusetts."

Curtis' eyes get a little bigger as soon as I tell him that.

"What brings you all the way up *here*? Well, maybe that's a silly question. Alright, son. You get some rest, and I'll wake you up in a couple of hours for breakfast. Then, we're gonna talk about rehab. Oh, and your phone is off, isn't it? We don't want them tracking you all the way up here."

I look over at my phone, which is on thirty-two percent battery.

"Uh, no... You *really* think the cartel, or even Malcolm or Ted could figure out how to track me?"

Curtis becomes flustered all over again.

"Is that a *serious* question, son?! YES! Of *course* they could! Turn it off! *NOW*!"

My nimble fingers quickly switch my phone to "off" mode.

"*Alright*, alright. It's off. Now what?"

Curtis grabs my phone.

"Now I take it and don't give it back to you until it's safe. Get some rest, Drew."

Feeling defeated, I lay down on my new hay bale mattress, grabbing extra straw around me to cover myself.

Despite the freezing cold, the next two hours of sleep are the best I've gotten in months. I *finally* have some hope for what's ahead, despite my fears.

# Anna - In her office, January 2018

It's Thursday, January eleventh, twenty-eighteen. Drew has been missing for almost three weeks. The last time anyone saw him was right before Christmas on Friday, December twenty-second, two-thousand and seventeen. I've been freaking out, not knowing where my brother is, along with the rest of the town.

Despite the town's interest in Drew's disappearance, I don't know how many townspeople *actually* care about his well-being. I think most of them just want to focus on something more terrible than their own lives.

As I look around at the lavender-colored walls of my office, I'm constantly reminded of Drew. This is where he stayed for *weeks* hiding from Malcolm and using. Then I kicked him out, and he stayed at his trailer not even two full nights before disappearing.

I *have* to make it my personal mission to find Drew and bring him back to Woodbank so he can get well. I would regret it for the rest of my life if I didn't at least *try* to save his life.

As I nervously pace around my office, thinking about all of the possible places Drew might be, I look down at the stack of mail on my desk. I brought it in hours ago but never bothered to look through it.

Amidst the pile of junk mail, I notice an envelope from "Jimmy Morris" with no return address. Could it be?! *No*—of course not. That was the fake name Drew insisted I call him when we played make-believe as kids. It was a tribute to the lead singer of his favorite band. Honestly, it might be him—what other *Jimmy Morris* would I know?!

I immediately tear open the envelope, pieces of white paper falling all around me. Inside is a letter.

Anna,

I want you to know that I'm okay. I'm sorry I didn't get in touch with you sooner. Curtis, the guy that's been letting me stay on his farm, took my phone away from me the day I got here. He threw me in rehab the next day, where I stayed for two weeks. Two whole weeks of being in a foreign environment where I had to celebrate Christmas and New Years with a bunch of strangers. I felt so alone. The first few days, I barfed my brains out. I couldn't eat a single thing. I would lay in bed at night shaking, not being able to sleep, my muscles and bones aching so bad I couldn't even get up. After that, I progressively got better, although I still had trouble focusing and would get anxious or depressed out of nowhere.

And I'm still not feeling like my old self. Detoxing sucks. Let's just put it that way, but it's worth it. I don't know what ever made me want to touch that poison in the first place, but I'm sure you'll scold me for that when I see you.

After three days of hell in rehab, I slowly started to open up in group therapy. The people there were great.

I'll tell you more about it some other time.

I know you have a lot of questions, but for now, I can only tell you that I'm safe and in good hands. Curtis and his wife Samantha have been putting me to work on their farm. It feels good to work hard with my hands and do something meaningful.

As much as they keep telling me that I'm helping them out, they're the ones who are really helping me. They're so kind and generous, and also tough. They're exactly what I need right now.

Anyway, Anna, we can keep in touch through letters, as long as you address them to "Jimmy Morris." I'll see you again when it's safe. Right now, things aren't too good for me. Malcolm, Ted, and the cartel are all looking for me. They want my head in exchange for the drug money I owe them. I'm going to make back the money here on the farm, and then I'll come home, I promise. Love you, Anna banana.

Jimmy

*WOW*—I knew Drew was alive! I could just sense it. He and I have always had a twin-like bond that nobody could ever understand. I'm *going* to find him.

# Anna - Interrogation Room, September 2018

"You're telling me that you knew your brother was alive back in *January*? And you didn't *SAY ANYTHING*?!"

Detective Paisley is *furious*. I run my hands through the ends of my straight, dirty blonde hair, not really knowing what to say next.

"I'm *sorry*, detective. I just wanted to protect him; he didn't even tell me where he was staying. Malcolm, Ted, and the cartel were all after him. I did what I thought was best at the time, and even *that* wasn't enough to keep him alive."

I'm starting to tear up as my face becomes red with heat. I look down at my lap, where my hands are cupped together, and start fiddling with my thumbs. A few seconds later, I look up at Paisley, who is not interested in showing me any sympathy at this point.

"You better start telling me *everything* you know, Ms. Abston, or we're going to have a problem."

A tear starts dripping down the left side of my face. I quickly rub it off as I decide to be more open with the detective.

"You have to understand, detective... Drew and I have always been close, ever since we were kids. And back in elementary school is when Drew's rage problems started to come about...."

Drew and Anna are eating lunch together alone in the cafeteria, as they do most days. Drew is in the fifth grade, and Anna is a third-grader. They're both typically loners, so they stick together as an unbreakable duo. Some days a friend or two will come join them at their table. That only lasts as long as Drew doesn't scare them off by getting into a fight with someone at school.

Drew is sipping his grape juice box until air pockets reveal the emptiness of its contents. Drew doesn't seem to care; he's going to continue sucking the straw until every last drop is consumed. Another fifth-grader looks over at him, annoyed by the sound.

"*HEY*! Knock it off, would you?! Your juice is obviously empty, man. Stop annoying everybody, *freak*."

The kid and his buddies who are sitting with him all chuckle as they stare back at Drew and Anna. Anna, in the middle of chewing her tuna sandwich, swallows her last bite quickly. She knows what is about to happen and wants to be emotionally prepared. Her brother Drew stands up, ready to knock some heads as he starts huffing and puffing.

"Mind your own business, Tyler, or I'll *knock* your teeth in, you egghead!"

The kid's head *is* slightly large and egg-shaped. Tyler stands up, wanting to look tough in front of his friends. He rolls his sleeves up.

"Oh *yeah*? You really think you could hurt *me*, you *WUSS*?!"

Anna stands up, ready to defend her brother.

"He's not a wuss, and he's not a freak either, *Tyler*! Leave Drew ALONE!"

Tyler laughs at Anna, which only makes Drew angrier.

"HA HA! You really think I'm gonna listen to *you*? A *third-grader*? Sit down, little girl. I'm about to—"

Drew throws the first punch at Tyler's left cheek before he can finish his sentence. He brings Tyler down to the ground, hitting his face repeatedly. Left hand, right hand, left hand, right hand. Anna steps in to stop the fight.

"DREW! *STOP*!!"

She grabs her brother by the back of his t-shirt and pulls him away from Tyler. Drew snaps out of his rage state, coming to his senses. He looks down at his bloody fists, mortified by what he has just done. Anna, scared by her brother yet again, starts to cry.

"You told me you would stop getting into fights, DREW! I can't believe you!"

She runs away in tears. Drew tries helping Tyler up off the ground, reaching out his hand.

"Listen, man. I'm sorry. I can get a little carried away sometimes."

Tyler stands up on his own, wiping the blood from under his nose.

"Stay *AWAY* from me, PSYCHO!"

Ms. Mulligan comes over to bring Tyler to the nurse's office, leaving Drew alone, astonished by his own actions. As all the other kids stare at him, he just stands there, not knowing what to say. About thirty seconds later, Mr. Green snatches Drew by the wrist, speedwalking him to the principal's office.

"Come with me, Mr. Abston."

*Here we go again.*

Detective Paisley interrupts my story.

"So you're saying you would always stand up for Drew when he got into trouble. Is that right, Ms. Abston?"

I yank my yellow cardigan down.

"Yes, that's what I'm trying to say. I've always felt this obligation to help Drew no matter what, even if I had to follow him into his darkness. So when he got into doing drugs and dealing, I worried about him *constantly*. I made it my mission to try to get him into rehab, and of course, he wouldn't listen. I couldn't sleep. I couldn't concentrate."

I take a deep breath.

"Worrying about Drew for months is what made me lose my job at the magazine because I could never get any work done. I regret letting him ruin my dream job. And when I finally heard from Drew after he had gone missing, he told me he had been in rehab for two weeks. Although it didn't end there, he still wasn't coming home because he was afraid for his *life*. And when the letters stopped in July, I knew something was wrong. He hadn't written to me in *two whole weeks*."

Detective Paisley stands up from his torturous wooden chair.

"Ms. Abston, this is very helpful information you've provided me with. I commend you for your bravery; I know it's not easy opening up about your brother's past. I'll see you soon."

I'm surprised with myself for sharing as much as I did today. At this point, I would do *anything* to find justice for my brother.

# Lisa - Outside of Benny's Alley, November 2017

The stars are so majestic above my mediocre job at Benny's Bowling Alley. Even though I can only partially see their beauty against the blaring lights of Benny's neon sign, they still bring me so much peace. As I light a cigarette and take a drag, I contemplate everything that's been going on in my life recently; it all starts to melt away. All of the stress between Drew and me doesn't seem to matter anymore.

I know I don't *have* to work here at this crappy job picking out bowling shoes for bratty kids, but I *need* independence from my parents. They can't control me anymore with their money and great expectations. Maybe I don't *want* to be a pharmacist like them.

I've already seen how much drugs can screw up the people I care about, even Malcolm. This guy is *selling* drugs with *my* boyfriend, *dangerous* drugs, and yet I'm friends with him. Perhaps the fact that I'm bored of my prim and proper upbringing made me addicted to danger? Drew and

Malcolm are both sweet guys underneath their psychotic tendencies (which I *love*, apparently). Speaking of which, here comes trouble.

Malcolm walks up to me in the darkness of the night during my fifteen-minute break.

"Hey, chica. What's shakin'? Can I get a drag of that?"

Malcolm snags the cigarette right out of my hand before I can even offer it to him.

"*Sure*, I guess."

Malcolm blows out a cloud of smoke to the left of him.

"Hey, Lis, you know how Drew has been acting so crazy lately? And how he's gone off the deep end with his addiction?"

I nod slowly, trying to understand where Malcolm is going with this.

"*Yeah*... so what's your point?"

Malcolm smirks, looking pleased with himself.

"Well, I was thinking... you and I hit it off so well, and I could take care of you. Why do you need *Drew* anymore?"

Annoyed by Malcolm's advances, I look down to the left at the concrete sidewalk.

"Malcolm, we've been *over* this. I think you're great, really. You're cute, you're funny, you're *insane*—everything I could ever want in a guy. But I'm gonna try to make things work with Drew. He needs help, and as his friend, you should be doing everything you can to get him *away* from drugs. I don't like what you guys do. As exhilarating as it is that you guys work in a dangerous field, I can't watch Drew suffer like this anymore. He should've *never* become friends with you in the first place senior year. I knew it from the moment you guys started talking in English class that you were bad news."

Malcolm inches toward me despite my lengthy speech that consisted of insults and turning him down.

"*Come on*, Lis. You knew you liked how bad I was when I moved to Woodbank senior year. You were just upset because you were already taken before I got here. You and I—we're the ones who're really meant to be. We would make such a good couple. You, a logical, *caring* woman, and me, an adventurous, artsy *man*. You need a real man in your life,

Lisa. I would be there for you no matter what, and I'd never stand you up for a date."

Malcolm is all up in my face now, brushing my hair behind my ear as I turn away from him. As much as I'm trying, I can't resist his charm. I look straight into Malcolm's eyes; he's only a few inches away from my face.

"I love you, Lis."

Malcolm closes his eyes and gently presses forward into my lips.

About thirty seconds later, I stop the kissing and push Malcolm off of me.

"MALCOLM—we can't do this!"

I burst into tears as Malcolm's confusion grows.

"Why *not*, baby? There's magic between us, you know it."

I look around, paranoid, to see if anyone just witnessed our kiss. Of *course,* Anna Abston is staring right at us from two rows away in the parking lot. You've *got* to be kidding me. She hurries away as soon as we make eye contact.

"Malcolm, I have to get back to work. We'll talk about this later, okay?"

Malcolm accepts my wishes and leaves, smiling at me as he walks away.

"*Okay*, I'll talk to you later, Lis. And I'll be thinkin' about you."

I am in *so* much trouble.

# Drew - Music class, Junior Year, March 2012

"Check this out, Mrs. H!"

I quickly run to the corner of the room, where a blue electric guitar typically sits untouched. I grab it and shred, trying to impress the teacher. Isabel giggles as she always does at everything I do.

"*Very* nice, Drew! Now let's get it together, everyone. We need to be ready for the Spring Concert, which is only *two months away*!"

Isabel reaches up to whisper in my ear. She's shorter than me by about a foot, so she has to *really* make an effort to get on my level. I'm a nice guy, so I meet her halfway and lower my head a little.

"She needs to take something and *chill*."

I cackle as I always do from Isabel's perfect comedic timing.

"I know, *seriously*. The concert is so far away, I don't know what her problem is."

Isabel gently nudges my arm with her elbow.

"Yeah, plus you can own *all* of us with any one of these instruments, you musical *freak*."

I may be naturally gifted at music, but I don't like to brag.

"Ha—that *might* be true. You're pretty great at the tambourine, though, Iz."

Isabel laughs.

"Ha, yeah... I'm not too shabby."

I lower myself to Isabel's ear, all while facing Mrs. Hilberry to at least *act* like I'm paying attention to her lecture.

"Anyway, Iz, you wanna get coffee after school today? We could meet at Reggie's, our usual spot."

Isabel blushes then smiles as if she's in a dream state.

"Sure, Drew. That sounds like fun."

I smile back at Izzy, my good friend of five years.

Later on, at the diner, I walk in and see Isabel waiting for me, sitting in one of the faded red booth seats that face the entrance. I walk over and hug my old pal.

"*Hey*, Izzy. What's goin' on?"

Isabel hands me a menu.

"Not much, just chillin', waiting for you."

I look down at my phone to check the time.

"Uh, *I* was on time. You're five minutes early."

I shake my head, smirking at Isabel.

"You're always trying to make me feel *bad*, aren't you, Izzy?"

Isabel smiles cunningly while flipping through her menu.

"Maybe, maybe *not*, Abston."

I roll my eyes.

"Anyway, Isabel, I wanted to talk to you about Rick. He's into you, *right*?"

Isabel is caught off guard. Her eyes widen as she continues flipping through her menu anxiously.

"*I don't know*. You're the first one to tell *me*."

I reach for Isabel's hand across the table. She's so beautiful. I love the way her wavy, caramel brown hair brushes the top of her shoulders perfectly. And her light blue eyes energize as well as soothe me.

"Well, I just wanted to let you know I sorta have feelings for you too. Is that *alright*? Or is that creepy?"

Isabel is beaming.

"*Reaaally*? I never thought *you* would be into me, Drew."

I gaze into Isabel's delighted eyes.

"Yeah, well, I've been thinking about our friendship *a lot* lately and how we work so well together. You're constantly making me laugh so hard I think my side is gonna split open. Plus, you're always there for me, even when I get a little crazy and decide to knock someone out."

I put on a British accent to make Izzy laugh.

"So, whatta ya say, Iz? You wanna give your ol' chum Andrew a chance?"

Isabel cackles at me, as usual.

"*Wow*, Drew. Um... *sure*!"

"Awesome. Let's start now. Consider this our first official date."

"Alright, Drew. You got it."

After about an hour of talking and making each other laugh, Lisa Yantz walks over to our table.

"Hey, Drew. Hey, Isabel. What are you guys doing?"

Although I'm having a great time with Isabel, who is *so* beautiful, I'm caught off guard by Lisa's stunning good looks. I'm such a bad person. Snapping out of the spell Lisa always puts on me, I look back over at Izzy, who is continuously smiling at me.

"*Oh*, hey, Lisa. We're on a date, actually. What are you up to?"

Lisa opens her mouth in shock, then smiles at Isabel and me.

"Well, well, well. You two *finally* got together, huh? That's great for you guys; you make such a cute couple. Alright, I'll leave you guys to it. Catcha later!"

Now that Lisa's gone, I can finally enjoy my time alone with Isabel in peace.

# Rick - Walking out of AP Chemistry, March 2012

Drew and I are both on our way out the door from AP Chemistry, trying to get out at the same time. It's an awkward moment since we haven't spoken in two weeks, not that we've really been talking for the past few months anyway. Drew snatched my crush of *two years* before I even had the chance to tell her how I felt. I don't know *what* his problem is. And even before he stole Izzy from me, Drew had been acting so weird, drifting away bit by bit.

He had done that in the past, not showing up to hang out at my house out of nowhere, ignoring my texts, and ditching me for a different partner in science class, but this was different. Months went by when Drew would be flaky, and now *this*? Not talking to me for two weeks, probably because he's guilty about Isabel.

Drew can be such a great friend when he wants to be or whenever his *mood* allows him to be. I want to trust Drew and let him back in as my friend. I just don't know how to do it anymore; I'm getting *so* tired of forgiving him.

Drew and I bump into each other as we try to squeeze through the door frame simultaneously. I decide to be the bigger person and acknowledge Drew first.

"*Hey*, buddy. Looks like fate brought us together. How've you been?"

Drew rolls up his sleeves, like when he's about to fight someone. Thankfully, instead of applying brute force, he reaches in to hug me.

"*Hey*, Ricky. I'm sorry about everything with Isabel and for ignoring you."

I shrug my shoulders, noticing Drew's remorseful demeanor.

"It's okay, man. I was upset you didn't talk to me about it first, but if you and Izzy are happy, you have my blessing."

Drew smiles at me.

"Thanks, man. Yeah, we're good. Izzy's the best. Hey, you wanna meet at Reggie's later, all three of us, to smooth things over?"

I nod my head as I fiddle my hands around in my front jean pockets, trying to believe Drew's peace offering is genuine.

"Sure, that sounds good. I'll meet you guys later."

After my encounter with Drew, I followed him to see what he was up to. I didn't believe that he was truly okay because he does this all the time. Pretending to be happy, then disappearing for no logical reason.

I followed Drew to his next class, which was gym, not caring that I would be late for my class. Unfortunately, what I saw next was telling and made all of my suspicions that much clearer.

I watched as Drew walked up to Lisa, picking her up by her hips and bringing her close to his face, both of them grinning at each other. There wasn't any kissing, so I *guess* it was okay? Drew's always been a flirt. Next, I saw them holding hands, and I *knew* that wasn't right. I had to tell Isabel.

# Isabel - By her locker, March 2012

As I'm sorting through books in my locker, Drew walks up to me from behind. I turn around, excited to greet my boyfriend. I love seeing him in his red flannel shirt; it makes him look like an adorable lumberjack.

"*Hey*, babe!"

I reach in to kiss Drew; he hardly makes an effort to kiss me back.

"*Hey*, *Izzy*. We have to talk."

My heart sinks; I know what that means.

"It's been really fun dating you this past week; you're amazing, Isabel. You're gorgeous, smart, funny—but Iz—I have feelings for Lisa."

Drew lowers his head; he can hardly look me in the eyes anymore.

"I'm so sorry, Isabel. I hope we can still be friends. Your friendship means the *world* to me. Can you forgive me for being such a moron?"

I'm heartbroken, but I don't want to show it to Drew. I wanna be his friend no matter what. I could never lose Drew Abston. He means too much to me. A tear drips down the left side of my face; I quickly wipe it away.

"Really, it's okay, Drew. You mean a lot to me, and although I honestly thought this could work, I guess we're just too good of friends. Good luck with Lisa; you're really going above your paygrade with *that* one."

Drew reaches in to hug me, laughing.

"*Yeah*, you're right about that, Izzy. Thanks for forgiving me. I love you, Iz."

I *really* wish the first time Drew said "I love you" to me was with romantic intentions, but I'll take it.

"I love you too, Drew. I'll see you later. I've gotta get to class."

"Alright, Iz. Text me later, okay?"

I half-smile back at my friend, trying to play it cool.

"Will do."

As I'm on my way to English class, Rick comes up to me in the halls.

"Iz—I *have* to tell you something, but you're not gonna like it."

I look away from Rick, not interested in hearing more bad news.

"Ricky, I am *not* in the mood. Drew just dumped me for Lisa."

Rick stops me in my tracks by standing in front of me.

"He did *WHAT*?! Well, that's what I was gonna talk to you about, actually. I just saw Drew and Lisa flirting in gym class. He picked her up, and they were laughing together."

My heart starts beating a million miles a minute, and my whole body increases a degree in temperature.

"Are you *KIDDING ME*?! Drew just told me he has feelings for Lisa, and now I'm finding out he was doing something about it *before* he broke up with me?! I can't, I just can't, Ricky."

I sink down to the ground against someone else's locker halfway to English class. Rick sits down next to me.

"Are you *okay*, Isabel?"

My entire body begins to shiver as goosebumps develop on my skin. My rage has suddenly turned into depression.

"Not really, Rick. But I will be."

Rick doesn't know what to do with himself; he's all worked up.

"Do you want me to punch Drew for you? Because, *trust* me, I will. I'm not afraid of him."

Rick is so scrawny compared to Drew's built physique; I don't trust him to pick a fight with Drew without getting *seriously* injured.

"Just don't do anything to Drew, okay, Rick? I'll be fine. We can both forgive him, right? He needs us to be his friends. You never know what could happen to Drew; he randomly gets into fights and ditches us sporadically. I don't wanna see him go off the deep end one day. If we can just *be* there for him, he might be okay. Alright, Rick?"

Rick nods his head unwillingly.

"Okay, Iz. I can do that."

# Roger - The Abston House, September 2017

It's a *mess* in here—an emotional one. Rebecca, Anna, and I are all standing in the kitchen, talking about Drew. It's typical of Drew to cause drama in this household, but today, oh, *today* is different. Anna is crying as she clings to my wife.

"I can't believe they *fired* me, mom! What am I going to do?! I loved working for the magazine. Now my career is *OVER*!"

As Anna continues to sob, Rebecca glances over at me, dismayed and not sure what to do next. I have a pretty good idea of what needs to be done.

Instead of comforting my daughter as I probably should, I start a riot about Drew's recent behaviors.

"That boy's going to *PAY*! Just you wait and see."

Drew comes stumbling through the backdoor into the kitchen. I decide to confront my son first.

"*Andrew Abston*—you have some explaining to do! Not only did Anna get fired from her job because she was worried *sick* about you and your bad habits, but you had to go and *STEAL* from my business on top of it?!"

Drew is dumbstruck as he tries holding himself up against the kitchen counter.

"What?! I don't know *what* you're talking about, dad. Why would I *ever* steal from you?! What, are you paranoid or something?"

Drew chuckles, thinking he's hilarious, so I charge up to him, standing directly by his face. I'm about to strangle my own son in front of my wife and daughter.

"Look at me, Drew. This *isn't* funny. You're hurting the lives of those around you with your addiction; you're hurting your own family. Do you want that? Huh? *HUH*?"

I smack my own boy right across the face to knock some sense into him.

"*ANSWER ME*, ANDREW! Or I *swear* you'll never be allowed back in this house again! And you'll *NEVER* take over my business as long as I live!"

Drew wakes up from his drowsy state, finally ready to fight back.

"I DON'T WANT YOUR STUPID LANDSCAPING BUSINESS, DAD! I never *said* I wanted it! If you ever cared about what *I* wanted, you would know I love music and that I wanna open up a music store one day and teach lessons to people!"

Anna interjects, furious.

"Drew, you're never going to open up a business of your own if you don't get *CLEAN*! If you won't do it for us, why can't you at least do it for *yourself*?!"

She sobs some more. Now it's Rebecca's turn to scold Andrew.

"Andrew Abston, you *better* go to rehab. Look at what you're doing to your sister! She's been worried *sick* about you for months! And so have *I*! We just care about you, honey. *Please* get better. We want you to live a good life, son."

Rebecca embraces our son. As much as she wants to lay down the law, all she really wants to do is comfort Drew. That's all well and good, but I can't do that for him, not now. I can hardly even *look* at him, and it's been this way for months. It's my turn to speak again.

"Drew, you're going to pay back *every single cent* you stole from my business, whether you go to rehab or not. I'm not kidding. A man has to own up to his mistakes. That's all I'm going to say."

I'm done. Whether Drew comes up with the money or not, goes to rehab or not, I can't worry about him anymore; it's just too hard. He's on his own now.

# Rebecca - Gene Henry's House, September 2017

"About two weeks have passed since Anna, Roger, and I confronted Drew at our house. He says he'll be able to pay back the money he stole from the business, and I want to believe him. Drew went back to work at Frederick's Supermarket a couple of weeks ago, so that means sometime in the next week or two, he'll be able to pay Roger back. I just want my boy to get *better*, Gene. What am I supposed to do?"

Gene Henry, our long-time neighbor of ten years, stares back at me in his kitchen as we sip on cups of coffee at ten a.m. I feel welcome in this sand-colored room with a fruit wallpaper trim. Gene's late wife must've picked that out. About thirty seconds after I've vented to him, Gene conjures up something to say back to me, the desperate mother.

"Rebecca, I could teach that boy a lesson if you'd like. I could scare him after work one night and threaten him, pretend I'm his drug lord boss, or something like that. Wear a mask. Make it seem legitimate."

I find myself gasping, holding my palm over my mouth, disturbed by Gene's plan at first.

"*What*?! No, Gene! I could never do that to Drew. Or... *could I*? I mean, I wouldn't *actually* be the one doing it to him. You would. I say go for it—nothing else has worked."

Gene takes another sip of coffee, planning out his next move, I'm assuming.

"I'll go there tonight, when it's dark out, and wait for him to get out of work. He'll never see it coming when I approach him by his car. I have a gun too, yah know. I'll just bring my pistol and whip it outta my pocket when the time is right. It'll scare Drew enough to stop screwing around with drugs and get back to society."

All of a sudden, I stand up, bringing my empty coffee cup to the kitchen sink. As I begin washing my mug, I start to shake my head repeatedly.

"No, no, *no*. Gene, I can't let you do that. It's too cruel. Thank you, but I'm going to have to figure out another way to get my son back."

I'm not sure Gene Henry understands the true definition of justice. I know he's looking out for my family and me. I just wish he'd give Drew the benefit of the doubt like I do.

"Okay, Rebecca. I just can't see you and your family *suffer* anymore due to Drew's actions. I trust you'll figure it out on your own. Just know I'm always here for you if you need me to step in; don't hesitate."

In the back of my mind, I'll be keeping Gene's offer to spook Drew as plan B. Knowing Gene has my back brings me an odd sense of peace.

"Thank you, Gene; I appreciate it. I'll talk to you soon."

# Drew - Frederick's Supermarket, October 2017

I can't *believe* I stole money from my dad's business to buy drugs; I'm *such* a scumbag. I guess my sin wasn't too awful since the money was also for living expenses. I can hardly keep up with the bills and my addiction with the pennies I've been making dealing. It's all my fault, really, because I haven't been working hard enough. Malcolm's been selling everything I can't to make sure we don't fall behind.

After I scan yet *another* yogurt cup at the checkout line, I look over at the huge clock on the wall. Although the numbers are a little blurry and wavy, I can tell that my shift will be over in ten minutes.

After I leave Frederick's, I head over to the bank, the same bank where my dad's landscaping company has an account. This is the account I stole from almost a month ago. Since then, my dad has taken me off of the account, no longer trusting me with handling the books or finances for his company.

I make a withdrawal from my personal checking account in the amount of $300, which is fifty dollars more than what I stole (I'm trying to be a good guy). After counting the money in my hands, I secure the green paper in the inside pocket of my denim jacket.

I then head over to Bobcat Bar to celebrate my new responsible way of living before paying my dad back. At the bar, I don't run into many friendly faces. Malcolm and Ted Savona being two of them. I see them sitting by the bar; Malcolm has disappointment written all over his face, like he doesn't want to see my face right now. I try looking at the two of them, but it's difficult when the yellow and red neon signs behind them are blinding me, even though they're not that bright.

"*Hey*, Drew, what are you doin' here, buddy? Shouldn't you be off pushing? You're *way* behind schedule, man. Cartel wants our product sold by the end of the month. You know the drill. And I can't keep pickin' up the slack for you."

Ted backs Malcolm up like a good little uncle.

"Yeah, *Abston boy*. Get your act together, or you might get an unfriendly face showin' up at your place one of these days."

Ted snickers, then takes a swig of his beer, staring me down with his maniacal glare. I decide to swing back verbally.

"Mind your own business, Ted. This has *nothing* to do with you."

I signal my hand towards my good ole middle-aged friend behind the bar.

"Hey, Allen, can I get a drink?"

Ted stands up and gets right up in my face.

"You better watch who you're talkin' to, boy. I'm not a very forgiving person. And my boy Malcolm here, he deserves the same respect *I* do, maybe even more. He's put his neck out on the line for you since you started sellin' together, Abston. Malcolm's always gone above and *beyond* what's expected of him; that's why he's gonna go far in life. You, on the other hand? HA! You're nothing but a piece of *trash*, boy."

Ted turns around and walks back to his seat, shaking his head and laughing with Malcolm. That's when I deal the first blow.

*SMACK*! Right to the back of the head.

I knock Ted Savona out in one single punch. I'm not usually this strong, not like how I used to be. Adrenaline must've kicked in. Malcolm looks down at his uncle's face against the floor, completely appalled by my actions.

"WHAT IS YOUR *PROBLEM*, DUDE?!"

Malcolm then takes a swing at me, to his misfortune. I may be weaker than I used to be, but Malcolm is still a puny little punk when he's been drinking. Unable to duck in time, I take the first hit to the right side of my face, blood squirting off the side of my mouth where my teeth puncture the flesh.

I then reposition my grip for the next punch. My super strength kicks in again, and I begin throwing punch after punch to Malcolm's face and then to his gut. Next, I tackle him down to the old creaky wooden floor, putting him in a chokehold, where he strains his voice begging for mercy.

"Stop it, Drew! *PLEASE*!"

Coming to my senses, I release my arms from Malcolm's neck. Allen, the bartender, comes running over from behind the bar. Enraged, he breaks up the fight.

"CUT IT OUT, BOYS! I can't *believe* I'm seeing this. Both of you—*OUT*!"

After Allen literally tosses us outside into the bitter cold rain, Malcolm looks up at me, filled with hatred. He touches his bottom lip, which is bulging and bleeding.

"Drew—just STAY AWAY FROM ME. I don't wanna see your face for a while."

I'm just standing there staring back at Malcolm, taking deep, heavy breaths as I cool off in the rain from my manic episode.

"*What* is your problem with me, Malc? We used to be buddies. I know I've been slacking on the sales lately, but what else about me has been *bugging* you so much? I don't get it!"

Malcolm holds his bruised left elbow as he stands bent over, not looking so great.

"I just can't stand the fact that Lisa wants to be with *you* of all people and not me. It's not fair that she met you first, man. You two started dating before I even moved to Woodbank. Why can't you just give her up already? You two don't even hang out anymore, anyway. Lisa and I have such great chemistry. And I think I could really make her happy, Drew. I'm sorry, that's just how I feel."

My eyes widen in disbelief.

"*Wow*, I had a feeling you were into Lisa based on all the looks you give her. Plus all the jokes you make about stealing her, but *man*, I didn't actually expect this to be real. Malc, you *know* I love her. We're gonna get married one day. Things might be rough right now, but I'm gonna get my act together for her."

Malcolm struggles to stand up straight, his face straining from the pain.

"That's fair, but I can't promise my feelings for Lis will ever go away. Let's just keep this partnership strictly professional. I don't think I can be friends with you right now, Drew."

I don't have any strength left to fight for this dying friendship.

"*Alright*, whatever you want, Malc. I'll catch you later. Sorry for kicking the crap out of you."

Malcolm brushes his hand in my direction, dismissing me.

"Yeah, yeah, whatever. See you around, Abston."

After my quarrel with Malcolm, I decide to finally pay my dad what I owe him. Walking into the Abston house again after everything I've done isn't easy. No one is home but my father, who is sitting at the kitchen table while sipping on some afternoon tea and reading the newspaper.

My father loves his Earl Grey tea breaks when he's off from work or at home on the weekends. Today he took off so he could get his money back from me in person. My dad looks up from his newspaper with reading glasses halfway down his nose.

"*Hey*, dad. How's it going?"

My dad's mood seems to be pretty neutral.

"I'm alright, son. I'm just happy that you decided to finally join me."

Of *course* my dad couldn't get through today without saying something sarcastic.

"*Really,* though, I appreciate you meeting me in-person to pay me back. I know I don't say this often, but

I'm proud of your character, Drew. Even though you've shown *extremely* poor judgment this past year, getting involved in drugs and whatnot, I have to give credit where credit is due."

My anxiety level has decreased a degree, knowing my dad isn't furious with me anymore.

"Thanks, dad; it means a lot that you approve of me. I honestly never felt that approval from you over the years while growing up in this home or in our home in Connecticut."

My dad seems slightly offended. I can tell by the way his forehead wrinkles contract above his nose.

"What'd you mean? Are you saying you're *ungrateful* for everything I've given you and your sister? Because if that's the case, you can have your money back, Drew. I don't want it."

Dad stands up and slaps the thin stack of cash right back into my hand.

"DAD! *What are you talking about*?! I never said I was ungrateful! You always do this; I say one thing trying to be honest with you, and you turn it into something completely different! How are we supposed to have a relationship if you're so hostile towards me?!"

After pacing around the kitchen for a minute with his hands on his hips, fuming, my dad finally stands still. As he leans towards me, he grips the chair in front of him so tightly I can see the veins popping out of his hands. In a few short seconds, that chair might be flying toward my body. He's never thrown anything at me or hit me before, but I have a feeling today might be the day.

"How are we supposed to have a *relationship*? Is that *really* what you're asking?! I can't have a son in my life that does drugs and deals drugs, Andrew! You don't want this life; I've seen it ruin far too many. And now my *own son's* life is being ruined too?! I won't stand for it anymore, DREW!"

My dad points towards the door with all his might. He's never been this serious before.

"GET *OUT*! I DON'T WANNA SEE YOUR FACE!"

I am *genuinely* afraid of my father at this moment, so I bolt out the back door as fast as I can.

After leaving the Abston house, I stand up against the house to the left of the door, gathering myself by taking a few deep breaths before I return to my trailer.

As much as I want to leave right away, something is telling me I should stay a few more minutes. I've got to peer into the house I used to live in because this may be my last shot. I don't know if I'll ever be welcomed back here again.

I notice my dad sitting at the kitchen table with his hand on his forehead, pushing back his messy, salt and pepper hair. He's crying, something I've never seen him do before. I thought my dad was a man of steel, a man so tough he could never get sad. Seeing that *really* throws me off; I don't know what to think of him anymore. At least he's human?

Before he sees me and I anger him any further, I run home as fast as I can. I'm not sure how many people are still on my side. It feels like I'm running out of allies. Maybe it's time to score again from my own supply.

# Drew - The Farm, March 2018

I've been here on the farm for over two months. In six months, I should be able to pay the cartel back and come back home to Woodbank. I wonder what everyone will think of me when I come back home, clean for the first time in a while.

I wonder if Lisa is waiting for me or if she decided to be with Malcolm at last. The very thought of them being together infuriates me to my very core, but I have to stay focused on my sobriety and working on the farm. While I was in rehab, they told us we should make amends with people for the things we did to them while under the influence. I've definitely done a *lot* to hurt those who love me.

Isabel, for instance—although I wasn't on drugs then, I regret breaking her heart in high school. It wasn't right of me to lead her on when I had stronger feelings for Lisa. And Rick, I always knew he liked Isabel, but I had to steal her from him anyway; I couldn't just let him have her. *Man*, I'm so selfish.

As far as Lisa goes, I could have been a *much* better boyfriend to her. I put Lisa to the side while I was high and never prioritized the love of my life; I regret that the most.

And then there's Malcolm—as much of a crappy friend as he was to me, he was just trying to look out for me financially. And as much as he completely *sucks* as a person, that's the one good thing I have to say about him. The way I treated him as a business partner (even though what we were doing wasn't right) was crappy.

My mind wanders to memories of my mom—oh, my sweet mother. I've worried her since the day I was born. No son should put their mother through what I put mine. And Anna—she lost her *job* because she was so worried about me. My faithful-to-the-end partner in crime; I treated her like *crap*.

Then there's Roger Abston, the stoic family rock, never approving of me except for on rare occasions. I got my rage from him. Although I'm not proud of the way our relationship has regressed this past year, I can still be grateful for the moments we've had over the years. Working together at his landscaping company was pretty fun; we even shared a couple laughs.

I ponder my regrets about the people in my life as I dig a hole for a new evergreen tree in front of Sam and Curtis' home. They've let me stay here, free of charge, in exchange for working on their farm. They even pay me a decent amount for my troubles, which is all going *straight* to the cartel.

I truly hope this tree I'm planting lasts as long as my sobriety, because I have *no idea* what I'm doing.

Later on, after finishing my shift for the day, I settle back into my room in the attic of Curtis and Samantha's home. I notice an envelope on my end table, just waiting for me to open it.

It's from Anna. She addresses it to "Jimmy Morris" from "Suzanne Wilkerson." Immediately, I rip the envelope open.

Dear Jimmy,

I've been thinking about you a lot lately. I wish I could tell someone that you're alive, safe and sober. When can you come home? I need my older bro in my life, even though you drive me a little crazy.

Anyway, the cops have been looking for you. They keep coming to our house every other day asking questions. There's this detective, Robert Paisley. He's kind of sketchy. I don't know how to read him. He makes me feel so guilty every time he looks at me.

Other than the cops parading around looking for clues as to where you might be, everyone else in town has been acting so strange. They act as if they care about where you are, but really, they just want to hear that you're alive or dead and get it over with already. I think that's so messed up.

Lisa, the cheater, has been doting over me every time she sees me, obviously feeling guilty for what she did. Malcolm's a creep as usual. Isabel is freaking out, wondering where you are, and I think Rick is too. Gene and mom still meet for coffee every week, except for the first few weeks you were gone. I think mom thought Gene did something to you. Honestly, I thought he did too before I got your letter, which thank God I did.

Mom's been a mess, as usual, not knowing where you are, so you better get back home soon, Jimmy. Dad can't take it any longer either. As much as he tries to act like a tough guy, he's just not the same anymore. Something changed in him when you left. Now and then, I'll catch him crying in the kitchen late at night, but I don't let him see me. I don't want him to realize that I can see his weakness and vulnerability.

Just come home soon, Jimmy, okay?

I love yah,
Suzanne

Don’t worry, Anna. I’m coming home as fast as I can.

# Ted - Interrogation Room, September 2018

Detective Paisley is eyeing me up and down as I sit in my uncomfortable plastic seat. This thing's a piece of crap. No wonder they make it feel like hell in here, so people will talk. Well, I ain't talkin'. He's gonna have to try *real* hard if he wants to get anything outta me.

"Now tell me, Mr. Savona, why you thought it would be appropriate to *threaten* Drew's life?"

The detective is right up in my face now, smelling like a dried-up carrot.

"And don't you find it *suspicious* that you would threaten him on the night he *disappeared* of all nights? Hm? *HMM*?!"

This detective's gettin' a little too freaky for my liking. I anxiously scratch my white beard, then run my hand through whatever gray hairs I have left on my head.

"I don't know what to tell you, detective. I was just stickin' up for my boy, Malcolm. He worked real hard to start a business with Drew, and Drew didn't even *appreciate* it. That Abston boy was always trouble, gettin' into fights and breaking girl's hearts. So why is it that *I'm* in the wrong for standing up for my family?"

All at once, Detective Paisley stands up, slamming his hand on the table.

"YOU THREATENED A DEAD MAN'S LIFE, TED! OF *COURSE* YOU'RE IN THE WRONG! You have no *idea* how miserable I could make your life. I could solve this case right now if I wanted to and lock you up for the rest of your days. So unless you wanna go to jail, you better start giving me some real answers, and *fast*."

Okay, now I'm scared. It takes a lot to scare me, but once I hear the word *jail*, it's all over.

"ALRIGHT, ALRIGHT! Yes, I threatened Drew's life on the night he disappeared, but I *swear* I didn't see him again after that! Drew and Malcolm were working for the cartel, dealing heroin for months. I'm sure you could look into that somehow. Don't you know who runs those operations and where they are?"

The detective is losing his patience with me.

"Don't you think I would've *found* Drew's killer by now if I could find the cartel?"

He bangs his hand down on the table yet again, then yells so loudly that spit spews into my face.

"STOP ASKING STUPID *QUESTIONS*!"

I wipe the droplets from my face onto my torn denim jacket, *disgusted*.

"Okay! Well, there's also Lisa, who was dating Drew, and she and Malcolm kissed. Maybe she killed Drew so she could be with Malcolm?! I don't *know*!"

I'll tell the detective anything if it means personal freedom for myself.

"All I know is that she and Malcolm are dating now and seem to be happier than two peas in a pod. Or—or maybe it was that sister of his, Anna Abston. She and Drew were real close, and it seems to me that Drew ruined her life when she got fired from that magazine she worked for. Maybe she wanted *revenge* or somethin'."

Detective Paisley appears to be content for the time being.

"I'll look into that. Thank you, Mr. Savona. You may go now."

He motions his hand towards the exit, and I take the opportunity to enjoy my freedom while I still have it.

# Curtis (with his wife, Samantha) - Interrogation Room, September 2018

My wife and I are calmly sitting across the table from an eccentric yet poised detective. Robert Paisley is a man on a mission to find Drew Abston's killer. He's so good at his job that it makes him a little unhinged at times. Noticing his character, Sam and I will answer all of our questions calmly and honestly because we have nothing to hide.

"Let me get this straight—Drew just *happened* upon your farm the night he left Woodbank? And neither of you knew who Drew was before that night, is that correct?"

Sam responds before I get a chance.

"Yes, that's correct, detective. The boy was in dire need of our help, so we took him in and sent him to rehab. He needed to get well before he could start working on our farm."

I fill in the rest of the details.

"Exactly what my wife said, detective. We didn't know Drew before that night. I gave him a hard time and took his phone away from him once he mentioned the cartel was after 'em. He also mentioned something about his friend Malcolm being angry with him, as well as Malcolm's uncle, who threatened to kill him."

Detective Paisley doesn't look surprised.

"Yes, that part I'm aware of; we're still looking into that threat. Is there anything else I should know about Drew's stay on your farm leading up to his death? Any *strange* behaviors?"

I think back to the night when Drew started acting *exceptionally* paranoid.

"I remember one night, Drew took it upon himself, for whatever reason, to take his phone back from my nightstand drawer. That was where it all went wrong, detective. Once that phone was turned back on, *anyone* could find Drew."

Detective Paisley has reached a revelation in his case.

"*Really*? And who might have found Drew, do you think?"

This is the part where I never found out what happened to Drew.

"All I remember was hearing Drew on the phone with somebody that night, on... what was it?"

Samantha interjects.

"July 17th."

"Thank you, honey. Yes, it was on July 17th. I woke up to Drew talking pretty loudly, so I went up to the attic to check on him. I caught him saying goodbye to someone on the phone, so I snatched it from him and immediately turned it off again. I guess that wasn't enough because whoever pinged Drew's phone must've hacked into his phone records and found out where he made his last call."

Detective Paisley slowly nods his head, hungry for more.

"I understand you were just trying to protect Drew from the cartel, which was *very* brave of you and Samantha to do, Curtis. Is there anything else you can remember after he made that call? Did you see anyone come to your house and take Drew away?"

Sadly, I can't help the detective any further.

“I’m sorry, detective. Sam and I were sleeping the night Drew was kidnapped, which was the night after he made that call. My guess is the cartel took him, but honestly, it could’ve been anybody. We really didn’t know Drew too well, his past at least. Didn’t wanna ask too many questions and trigger him because he was still a recovering addict, you see.”

Samantha seems eager to share more.

“Yes, Drew was *so* sweet and grateful. We had dinner together every night and played card games afterward. He worked so hard for us, and, detective, if he just had a little more time, I *know* Drew would have been able to pay the cartel back. Then maybe he would still be alive...”

Sam bursts into tears; she loved that boy as if he were her own. I rub my hand against my wife’s back as I explain her anguish to the detective.

“We were never able to have children of our own, detective. So you see, that’s why we’re so heartbroken over Drew’s death.”

Detective Paisley shows sympathy for my wife and me.

"You did all that you could for Drew. Don't beat yourselves up. As you said, it could have been *anyone* that killed Drew, and that's what I'm going to find out."

# Anna - Drew's Trailer, December 2017

I'm finally braving it out and am going to tell Drew about Lisa and Malcolm's kiss. I don't want to send him spiraling into his addiction, but he deserves to know the truth. I gently tap at Drew's front door, trying not to startle him at two-thirty in the afternoon. I never know when my brother is sleeping these days.

*Knock Knock*

Drew opens the door, looking exhausted as usual.

"Yo, what's up, Anna banana? Why are *you* here?"

I scoff at my older brother.

"It's nice to see you *too*, Drew. Can I come in?"

Drew looks behind him, checking the status of his place, which I'm sure isn't very tidy.

"*Yeah*, sure. Come on in, sis."

Upon entering Drew's trailer, I pull out a stool by his mini kitchen counter and take a seat. I then watch as Drew fumbles around in his kitchen, looking for something to offer me. Despite the fact that my brother's a mess right now, he still manages to be hospitable, and that's impressive.

"You want anything to drink? I could put on a pot of coffee or something."

"Nah, that's alright. I already had some this morning."

As I survey Drew's trailer kitchen, I start to tear up, which he notices.

"Anna, are you *okay*? What's going on?"

I make eye contact with Drew for a split second, then immediately turn my head to the right, staring at the microwave.

"It's gonna be hard to look at you when I say this, Drew, so I'm not going to."

Drew is getting frustrated.

"What *is it*, Anna?!"

I lower my head.

"I saw Lisa and Malcolm kissing. You know, *actually kissing*, making out."

I now look up at Drew, whose eyes are welling up.

"I'm *so sorry*, Drew. I think they really have feelings for each other."

Drew yells at me as tears stream down his face.

"WHEN WAS THIS?!"

I stand up, no longer feeling at home in my brother's trailer.

"A few weeks ago outside of Benny's Alley. I saw them after I left Frederick's that night and was walking to my car."

Drew slams his hand down on the counter.

"AND YOU'RE JUST TELLING ME THIS *NOW*?!"

I walk toward my brother in an attempt to calm him down. Stupid, it seems, to walk up to an angry person, but I know my brother.

"Drew, *please* calm down. I hate seeing you like this!"

Drew pushes me away with both hands as I reach in to hug him.

"NO! Don't tell me to *calm down*, Anna! You should've told me right after you saw it happen!"

A saltwater droplet drips down my left cheek.

"I'm *sorry*, Drew! I know you're already struggling with your addiction, so I didn't wanna make things more difficult for you! I can see now that I should've told you sooner."

Drew collapses into my arms, hugging me as he sobs. A minute passes, and then he stands up again, wiping the tears from his puffy eyes.

"It's not your fault, Anna; it's Lisa and Malcolm's. I'm gonna kick the *crap* out of my so-called *best friend*, and when I'm done with him, I'm gonna *dump* that cheater! I should've never broken up with Isabel to get with Lisa back in high school. None of this would've *ever* happened."

Drew grabs his coat and rushes out of his trailer, leaving me with no choice but to yell after him.

"*Please* be careful, Drew!"

I don't know what's going to happen next, but I'm glad I told Drew the truth. I just hope he doesn't get the crap kicked out of him. Or worse, I hope he doesn't turn to his addiction for comfort. *What have I done*?

# Drew - Lisa's House, December 2017

Yesterday, I confronted Malcolm about him and Lisa cheating behind my back. Because I'm so weak from my addiction, he defeated me in my efforts to kick the crap out of him. I accepted defeat and took my supply home that night after Anna had already left. I just want my life back before drugs, before I became a shitty human being, started selling, and became an addict. I *really* wanna try to become a better person.

Today, I'm going to start by confronting Lisa. I don't know what I'm going to say to my girlfriend of almost six years, but I'm sure the words will come to me when I see her. Surprisingly, I'm not high. I want to be completely sober for our discussion.

I walk up to Lisa's front door in the middle of the day, knowing her parents aren't home.

*Knock Knock*

Lisa opens up the door about thirty seconds later.

"*Drew*? I haven't seen you all week! How're you doing, baby?"

She reaches in to kiss me, and I let her, yet I don't reciprocate.

"What's *wrong*, Andrew? Everything okay?"

I give Lisa the death stare.

"You know what, Lis? Everything is *not* okay. And you know *why*? BECAUSE YOU KISSED MALCOLM! Anna told me all about it, you lying slut!"

Lisa gets defensive.

"*Woah*! Wait a second, Drew! Malcolm kissed *ME*! And *sure*, I liked it, but nothing else happened after that, I swear! Later that night, he called me, and I told him I couldn't cheat on you with him. I told him that I loved *you,* and that was that. You have to *believe* me, baby."

I'm so sick of this fake "baby" crap from Lisa. I can't do this anymore.

"I know you're *in love* with him, Lisa! Don't pretend that you're not. I see the way you guys look at each other whenever we all hang out."

At this point, I'm flailing my arms around in a frenzy as I scream at Lisa.

"And I know you're sick of me; I'm nothing but a *DRUGGIE*. I GET IT!"

Lisa closes the door behind her, standing out in the cold with me without a jacket. She must *really* not want me in her life anymore. She grabs my right arm, trying to calm me down.

"DREW! You *have* to calm down. I don't wanna be with Malcolm! How many times do I have to say it?!"

She starts crying, which doesn't impress me.

"Lisa, I can see how upset you are, which tells me two things—that you care about me and that you care about Malcolm. I'm going to make this *real* easy for you, Lisa—go ahead and be with Malcolm. I'M *DONE*!"

And just like that, Lisa sprints into her house, not saying a word, just sobbing. I can tell this was the right thing to do. I mean, a girlfriend of almost *six years* doesn't chase after her boyfriend who basically broke up with her *for* her?

I gave her the option to be with Malcolm, and she took it without even having to say a word. I may be trying to hide my emotions, but I'm devastated. Lisa was my life for *so* long.

I've gotta get high; my back is killing me, and I feel a chill running up and down my spine that not even the December weather could provoke. A tear streams down the left side of my face as I think about what I'm about to do, yet I walk home to my trailer to do it anyway.

As soon as I get to my trailer, I grab a syringe, spoon, foil, belt, and lighter—my usual accomplices. Heating up the brown powder is a breeze to me at this point. Injecting it into my popped vein is a piece of cake by now.

That initial euphoric rush makes all the pain go away. I finally feel free, free from all the *crap* going on in my life. I need to get away from it all. Maybe *tomorrow* I won't need this vice to survive anymore, because one day, it's *going* to kill me; that I know for sure.

# Malcolm - Ted's Trailer, January 2018

It's late at night, almost eleven-thirty, but I don't care. I charge right into my uncle's trailer, slamming the door wide open in the midst of the freezing January weather. He deserves to suffer a little.

"What did you do, uncle?! *WHERE'S DREW*?! I haven't seen him in over two weeks! The longest I've ever gone without seeing or hearing from him was a few days. Last month I thought he was dead when he totally ghosted me for almost *three weeks* when we had product to sell. At *least* he texted me a few times while he was gone. This time is different. I haven't seen *or* heard from Drew in over TWO WEEKS! Did you *kill him*?!"

Uncle Ted doesn't like my accusations very much, which I can tell by the look of displeasure on his face. He talks back to me with his obnoxious country accent.

"What are you talkin' about, boy? I didn't kill that piece of crap! Sure, I roughed him up a bit for yah before he disappeared suddenly, but I'm glad I did! The kid was treating you like *trash*, Malcky. I did you a favor, and whoever *did* kill Drew knew what they were doing. That boy is the scum of the earth. You don't wanna go near people like that, nephew."

I shove my Uncle Ted into the wall next to his flat-screen TV, almost knocking it to the ground.

"Don't talk about Drew like that!"

My uncle pushes himself off the wall, straightening out his denim jacket.

"Oh, Malcky, I thought you'd be *happy* Drew was gone after he dumped Lisa! Now she's fair game, buddy."

I crack my knuckles.

"*Don't* call me buddy. And whatever happened between Lisa and me is over, at least for now. And it's *none* of your business! Stay out of my life!"

I make a break for it and run all the way to Lisa Yantz's house; I have to see her. If she keeps ignoring my calls and texts, I don't know what I'm going to do; she's the love of my life.

Finally, I get to the front door of Lisa's, texting her that I'm outside. I know she at *least* stays up until midnight, so she'll for sure see my text and come out.

A few minutes later, I notice a light turn on in the foyer of her house. I see Lisa walking downstairs in her pink and red heart pajamas, which is absolutely adorable. Lisa slowly opens the door with a perplexed look on her face.

"*Malcolm*? Why are you at my house so late?"

I reach my hand out and grab Lisa's.

"I just needed to see you, Lis. Have you heard about Drew?"

Lisa quickly pulls her hand away from mine.

"What *about* Drew? Did something happen to him?! Oh God, please tell me he's alive!"

On the inside, I wanna roll my eyes. She's *still* obsessed with him.

"I don't know, Lisa. All I know is he hasn't texted me in over *two weeks*, and I haven't seen him since. That's why I'm here. I wanted to tell you myself. I also wanted to tell you I'm here for you whenever you're ready to officially date. I know about Drew dumping you."

Lisa folds her arms in front of her.

"Malcolm, are you *serious*? I'm not ready to date you or *anyone* right now, especially since Drew is missing! He *is* missing, isn't he? His family must've filed a missing person report."

On the one hand, it's annoying how much Lisa still cares about Drew, and on the other hand, I care that he's missing too. Drew and I have had our ups and downs, the latter being more frequent lately, but deep down, I'll always care about the guy.

"I dunno, Lis. We better check with your ol' pal Anna."

I chuckle as Lisa gives me the death stare.

"Ha ha. Very funny."

All of a sudden, Lisa and I are headed out the door as soon as she grabs her shoes and coat.

"Come on, Malc. You wanna find Drew as much as I do, right?"

I'm not sure if I have much of a choice as Lisa grabs my arm and pulls me towards her car.

"Uhh, do we have to go right *now*? It's past midnight! I'm sure Anna is asleep already."

We get into Lisa's sleek, black four-door sedan, a twenty seventeen model, and she starts her car.

"Yeah, Malcolm. We're going *right* now! Drew could be in trouble, and we have to get ahead of this before—"

Lisa tears up as she starts driving toward the Abston house.

"—before it's too late, Malcolm."

I comfort Lisa by rubbing her shoulder.

"It's gonna be okay, Lis. We'll find Drew. I'm sure Anna knows something."

The next ten minutes of driving are filled with silence and bumpy roads with only the moon and headlights lighting our path.

# Anna - The Abston House, January 2018

I look over at my phone at twelve thirty-five in the morning. It's buzzing, and Malcolm's name is popping up on my screen. Begrudgingly, I answer.

"*Malcolm*? Why are you calling me so late?"

Malcolm sounds like he's right outside my house as he answers me.

"Anna! I'm outside of your house right now with Lisa. Please don't hate us. We just wanna know if Drew is okay. We haven't seen or heard from him in over two weeks. Do you know anything?"

I grab my lime green robe and get myself out of bed.

"I'm coming down."

As soon as I reach the last step and enter the foyer, I notice Lisa and Malcolm's sad faces at my doorstep. I wanna leave them out there in the cold for everything they put my brother through, but I'm bigger than that—I think. Time to open the door... here goes nothing.

"Come on in, you guys. Let's go to the kitchen, but we have to be quiet; my parents are asleep upstairs."

I flick on a subtle light by the coffee machine, maintaining a low profile for the three of us.

Lisa and Malcolm make their way into my kitchen and sit down at the old oak table. I'm standing, trying to show dominance in this situation.

"Okay, so here's what I know. On Tuesday, December fifth, I went to Drew's trailer and told him how I saw you two *kissing* back in November, outside of Benny's Alley."

Malcolm and Lisa look at each other, guilt overcoming both of their faces.

"As soon as I told Drew, he *flipped out*, and rightfully so. Then he told me he was gonna kick the *crap* out of you, Malcolm, which obviously didn't happen because of the state he was in. The day after that, on Wednesday, December sixth, I know he broke up with you, Lisa; again, it was justified."

I shift my weight from left leg to right leg as I organize my story.

"The day after that, on Thursday, December seventh, Drew came to my office in the middle of the day asking for a place to crash for a while. I didn't know a while meant nearly *three weeks*. It was just Drew and me in my office because I started leasing the space for my personal blog ever since he got me fired. Anyway, one day after a hard day of work, I *actually* witnessed Drew shoot up, and that was it for me. Usually, he would go into the bathroom for a while and come out high as a kite, so I assumed he was shooting up in there. This time, he must've accidentally left the door open because I walked past the bathroom and witnessed the needle go *straight* into Drew's restricted arm. I couldn't handle it. He needed to get out of my office at that *very* moment."

I look Malcolm straight in the eyes.

"I didn't care anymore if he had to face you, your Uncle Ted, or the cartel. I couldn't keep *enabling* him, so I kicked him out. That was on Thursday, December twenty-first, which was the last time I saw Drew. I know he was staying at his trailer again after he left my office because I ran into Isabel and Rick. They told me they were expecting to meet Drew at his trailer and bring him to rehab the morning of Saturday, December twenty-third. Apparently, he was gone, having left behind his lizard, Marty, which is *completely* unlike his character, even for the state he was in. Anyway, I'm just as worried as you guys are. I have *no idea* where my brother is."

Malcolm speaks up after my long-winded story.

"So that's where the scumbag was all that time, at your office, shooting up *my product*! I mean, *his* product, but we were business partners. It wasn't right for him to do that!"

Lisa feels as though she's allowed to speak now.

"No, it wasn't *right*, Malcolm, but can you *blame* him for everything you and I put him through?!"

Malcolm's getting worked up.

"Yeah, but you guys don't *get it*; the cartel's been asking me questions lately. Drew and I were supposed to give them a cut of our sales by the end of December, and I could only give them my half since Drew went MIA. I mean, I'm not *really* on the hook, but I'm definitely not on their good side. And as for *Drew*? Well, he's shit out of luck, ladies, I'm sorry to tell you."

I've had enough of Malcolm's negativity.

"*Alright*, Malcolm. I GET IT! He could be *dead* for all we know! But you need to remember that *you're* the one who got him into this mess! I could strangle you *RIGHT NOW* for everything you've done to my brother!"

I lunge towards Malcolm, overcome by wrath. Lisa tries to break up the fight, failing miserably as she gets tossed to the side. I kick Malcolm over in his chair and punch him in the face repeatedly on the ground, a signature Drew move. Malcolm throws a punch back, getting up off the ground. All of a sudden, the main light in the kitchen turns on, and my parents run toward me to stop the fight. My mom is in tears.

"*What are you DOING, Anna Elizabeth*?!"

My dad reaches toward me and pulls me back by both of my shoulders.

"*ANNA*! Stop this nonsense, *NOW*!"

My mom is livid.

"*Why are you two fighting*?! And in the middle of the night, of all the times, in *MY* home?!"

I look over at Malcolm, whose nose is bleeding. Lisa hands him a tissue out of her purse to stuff up his nostrils.

"I'm sorry, mom and dad, but I can't *take* it anymore! Drew is *missing*, and Malcolm and Lisa are here acting like they actually *care*?! Malcolm turned him into a drug dealer and is basically the reason Drew is an addict, and could be the reason why he's *dead*!"

I point my thumb in Malcolm's direction.

"And Lisa cheated on Drew with *this* guy after she was with my brother for *SIX YEARS*!"

I'm sobbing as I lean into my mom for comfort. My dad is in full force defense mode. He looks over at Lisa and then at Malcolm.

"You two—GET *OUT*! You've caused enough pain for my family. I don't wanna see your faces *EVER* AGAIN!"

Malcolm grabs Lisa's hand, and they bolt out of our home. I'm sick of them acting like they ever cared about my brother. I'll figure out where he is on my own. I don't need their sad, pathetic help.

# Rebecca - Gene Henry's House, February 2018

"How are we going to find *Drew*, Gene?!"

I start sobbing in Gene's living room as I sit on one of his floral sofa chairs.

"What if—if he's *dead*?!"

Tears stream from my face as I cover my eyes with my palms. Gene sits down on the matching floral chair across from me and hands me a tissue.

"We'll find him, Rebecca. Don't you worry. And when we do, you know that boy's gonna have to pay for all he's done to you and your family, *right*?"

I look up at Gene in shock.

"*What* are you talking about, Gene?"

Gene looks me straight in the eye, no remorse to be found.

"Oh, come *on*, Rebecca. Don't tell me you've never thought about it."

I look around the room, feeling guilt deep within and not understanding why.

"Thought about *what*?"

Gene's face becomes filled with a dangerous level of excitement.

"Teaching Drew a lesson! Roughing him up a bit, making him pay for the destruction he's brought down on the Abston name, that's what!"

I stand up, ready to leave as soon as possible.

"I mean, *yes*, I've thought about it, Gene. But that doesn't mean I would ever *act* on it! I could never do that to my son!"

Gene looks me in the eyes again, this time with a conniving glare.

"Are you *sure*, Rebecca?"

I pace around Mr. Henry's living room.

"Well, I guess if someone *else* did it, I wouldn't be *completely* in the wrong, right?"

Gene nods his head.

"Right."

I stop myself mid-pace and put my hand on my chin.

"What do you propose we *do*, Gene?"

Gene slowly walks over to his bookshelf, picking out a book to flip through as he comes up with a plan.

"I say we hire a couple of those slums from the trailer park where Drew was living to go beat 'em up really nicely. I'm sure those trailer trash teens would do *anything* for a quick buck. Besides, they were raised to be tough; it won't even phase them, *trust* me, Rebecca."

A myriad of thoughts come flashing through my mind. Do I want to find my son in a peaceful way and accept him back into our family as if nothing ever happened? Or do I want to teach him a lesson he'll never forget? About thirty seconds later, I come up with a response.

"Let's do it, Gene. Andrew could use a wake-up call. All he's ever been was trouble, and I've been enabling him his *whole* life. I forgave him for every wrong thing he did, every kid he beat up in school, every test he cheated on, dealing and foolishly starting to use drugs. Then, of course, he got Anna fired from her job and *stole* from the family business. I'm SICK of it, Gene! I just want my kind, sweet boy back because I *know* he's in there somewhere!"

Gene puts his hand on my shoulder for reassurance.

"I know you do, Rebecca. We'll get him back."

I smile at Gene, then start pacing around the room again, taking a blissful trip down memory lane.

"I would see glimpses of his kind, sweet soul whenever we would bake sugar cookies together during Christmastime when Anna was busy writing about celebrities. Ah, and I remember when Drew and I used to watch game shows together on Saturday mornings. And sometimes, he would play guitar for me and sing. I haven't heard his voice in *years*; his singing voice, of course."

All of a sudden, I stop pacing, realizing the urgency of the moment.

"Alright, that's enough reminiscing. Let's hire those kids to find Drew and teach him a lesson. I'll go down to the trailer park now and see who I can find to help. I'll put them in touch with you, Gene, so my husband doesn't get suspicious. I don't want to drag him into this because I know he wants to find Drew the *right* way. He's so rigid about rules and doing things a particular way."

I grab my coat and start walking towards the front door. I've got to get going before it gets dark out.

"Alright, Rebecca, be safe out there. You know some of those kids' parents have guns, *right*?"

I look back at Gene before I walk out the door.

"I'll be alright. Thanks, Gene."

# Anna - Reggie's Diner, March 2018

Oh, the strife of a sister living with a secret *no one* can know about for the sake of her brother's safety. Knowing her own brother is alive and not being able to tell a single soul—not even her own parents.

As I sit in my red, plush seat, sipping my coffee, I think back on the last letter I received from Drew on Friday. I've been getting a letter from Drew every week, which is usually delivered to me on Thursdays or Fridays. He seems happy, like he's found a real home where he's staying with the older couple.

I'm not allowed to know where or who Drew is staying with, just that he's okay and is having a great time. I'm *so* glad my brother is finally clean. I wish I could find him so I could see it for myself. I just *can't wait* until he's able to come home again.

Interrupting my pleasant thoughts is the sight of Lisa Yantz walking into the diner. Our last interaction at my house didn't go so well.

Lisa takes a deep breath, does the polite thing, and walks over to my table. I'm sitting at Drew's favorite booth, just one table away from the hostess station.

"*Hey*, Lisa. Long time, no see, huh? You and Malcolm ever get together?"

Lisa seems to be shocked by my implication.

"*Wow*, you cut straight to the chase, don't you? No, actually. Malcolm and I aren't a thing; we're not even talking right now."

I look at Lisa with judging eyes.

"And why is *that*, might I ask?"

Lisa takes a deep breath, letting out a long exhale.

"Because Malcolm doesn't seem to care that much about finding Drew. I don't know, maybe I'm just paranoid, maybe it's—"

I complete Lisa's sentence for her.

"—an *instinct*. That's what it is, Lis. If you can't trust him, then you can't trust him. I don't blame you."

Lisa feels comfortable enough to sit down in the booth seat across from me.

"Yeah, I can't be with someone like that. Plus, I can't be with *him*, not after everything I put Drew through. And I still care about Drew. I *really* love him, Anna; you *have* to believe me."

I tap three fingers on my coffee cup as I sit slouched down in my seat. Reluctantly, I put my trust in Lisa.

"I believe you, Lisa."

Lisa's eyes light up.

"*Really*? You *do*?"

I sit up, bringing my hands together and interlocking my fingers.

"Yeah, sure. But you know what *really* bothers me? How you and Malcolm are basically the reason he's missing. You can love someone and not be good for them, Lisa. And you know *what*? I'm sick of hearing you profess your love for my brother. He deserves *better* than you and Malcolm. And I'm going to find him and bring him home. Just you wait and see."

Lisa gets up, sick and tired of my accusations, I'm sure. Oh well, truth hurts.

"I'm *out* of here, Anna. I thought we could have a mature conversation about Drew, but I should've known better. Let me know when you're ready to act like an adult."

As Lisa is walking toward the exit, I yell back at her like a child, proving her point further.

"*YEAH*, WELL, HAVE A NICE LIFE, LISA!"

Everyone in the diner is staring at me after my outburst. They all quickly look away after they realize who I am: the sister of a possibly dead kid. Little do they know he's alive.

After sitting and sipping for about twenty minutes, I finally leave the diner. On my walk home, I contemplate what Drew has gotten me into. I'm lying to *everyone* about not knowing if he's okay or not. And he gets to be happy on some farm while I'm stuck here in *Woodbank*, picking up the broken pieces of his life?

Not only did Drew get me fired from my job at Woodbank Magazine, but he also made me watch him slowly decay in my office while he hid from the world. And now he's hiding *again*! When will I stop enabling him?!

Maybe I'll go home and do some research on farms in the tri-state area. I *have* to find Drew and end this madness.

# Malcolm - In his trailer, April 2018

*KNOCK KNOCK KNOCK*

I open the door to my trailer, and of *course*, there stands Lisa Yantz. I knew she would come back.

"*Hey*, beautiful. I knew you couldn't resist seeing me. What took you so long? Why haven't I seen or heard from you in *three months*?"

Lisa walks right up to me and presses her lips into mine.

"*Woah*, girl! Hold on a minute. Could we catch up first before you start mauling my mouth?"

Lisa seems on edge, yet she puts on a smile.

"*Yeah*, I don't know, Malcolm. I've just missed you is all. And I know the whole Drew being missing thing was coming between us, and I just don't want it to anymore. Is that *okay*?"

I can't stop myself from smiling.

"*Yeah* it's okay! I'm happy to see you, *Lis*. I've missed you too. Any word on where Drew might be?"

Lisa sits down by my tiny kitchen counter.

"*No*, still nothing. It's depressing, actually. I just wanna make sure he's *safe*, I don't know...."

Lisa looks off to the right, gazing at my couch in the living room.

"*Hey*, Malcolm, do you wanna play some video games or something?"

Lisa walks into my living room.

"Remember we all used to do that together? You, me, and Drew. We had *fun*, didn't we? Before everything got—you know, messy."

I'm stunned by what I'm hearing. Is Lisa *for real*?

"Lisa, are you sure you wanna hang out? You seem pretty caught up thinking about Drew. I thought you wanted to be with *me*."

Lisa storms back into the kitchen, fury written all over her face.

"Are you *serious*, Malc? You can't even think about your *missing* friend for *one second*?!"

Lisa gets right up in my face, backing me up against my kitchen sink. I do a one-eighty and jump away from her, surrendering my hands in the air.

"*Woah*, Lisa! Take a chill pill. I didn't say I couldn't *think* about the guy. I'm just talking about *us—you* and *me*. Is it okay if I do that every once in a while?"

I lower my hands, walking close enough to Lisa so I can grab her hand. As usual, she can't resist my charm.

"You and me, we've got *chemistry*, babe. Do you really wanna throw all that away because our friend is missing?"

Lisa looks dreamily into my eyes as we lift our interlocked hands towards each other.

"*No*, I wasn't *saying* we couldn't talk about us. I just don't know if I can while Drew is still *missing*, Malcolm!"

I drop Lisa's hands and turn away. She walks over to me again, noticing the dismal look on my face.

"That doesn't mean we can't still *see* each other, Malcolm. We can hang out again like we used to; remember how *fun* that used to be?"

My dreary mood has subsided. I smile at my future beau.

"*Okay*, sure. As long as we can still see each other, that's enough for me, Lis."

Lisa is so ecstatic with my response, she wraps her arms around my torso and squeezes me.

"Oh, that's *great*, Malcolm! This makes me so happy. You have no idea."

As Lisa is suffocating my rib cage, I think about how I'm going to pull off a relationship with her. She's *never* going to be with me as long as Drew is still around. So the solution is simple: I'm going to have to find and kill Drew Abston.

# Lisa - Reggie's Diner, May 2018

About a month has passed since Malcolm and I decided to be *just* friends until we find Drew. I have to say, it's been *really* difficult hanging out with him and not being his girlfriend. Sometimes I wish I'd never met Drew so I wouldn't have to feel so guilty about my feelings for Malcolm.

Sitting here at Reggie's Diner, sipping my tea, I ponder my romantic future. I'm having a great time by myself until, of course, Isabel and Rick from high school walk up to my table.

Isabel has a huge smile on her face as she and Rick are holding hands.

"*Hey*, Lisa. How's it going?"

Rick greets me too.

"Hey, Lisa."

I fold my hands together, sitting up straight in my seat.

"I'm doing alright. Drew's *still* missing, so there's that. I honestly don't know what to think anymore. My best guess is he fled to avoid the cartel since, you know, he owed them money and everything."

Rick and Isabel look surprised as if they don't already know this about Drew. Rick shifts his stance uncomfortably.

"Yeah, honestly, I didn't know he owed money to anyone. I could've helped him out. I even offered to get him in on a solar panel company my buddy started up. We were gonna meet here, actually, the night before he disappeared. I wonder why he never showed."

This sort of information doesn't surprise me.

"I mean, Drew was *always* flaky, you both know that. He meant well, and he really wanted to change for the better. I *know* he did. Drew wanted to make something of himself, but he was never capable of actually doing it. One minute he was up—happy, involved with his friends and family, caring, always there for you. And then, the next moment, he would flip like a dime, and no one would be able to get in touch with him. And of course, the drugs made him even *worse*, and—"

Isabel abruptly cuts me off mid-sentence.

"*Don't* talk about *Drew* like that, Lisa! He's a good guy, and we have to give him the benefit of the doubt! Obviously, Drew's always had problems, and we all should've made more of an effort to help him. I'm just as guilty of not reaching out to Drew when I should've all these years. I was really hurt when he dumped me for *you*, Lisa, *and* I was incredibly jealous."

Rick is looking at Isabel with both bitterness and adoration laced into his expression. I lay back in my seat.

"Alright, Isabel. I understand where you're coming from. I just get so *frustrated* sometimes, yah know?"

Rick offers words of wisdom for us all.

"We have to stay hopeful that Drew is alive, you guys. And when we *do* find him, we have to give him a second chance. Drew deserves to be forgiven for all he's done to us because when it comes down to it, he really hurt *himself* more than anyone else."

Isabel turns to her boyfriend, kissing him on the cheek.

"*Dang*! I didn't know you could be so *sappy*, Ricky. Hey, let's get a table, okay?"

Rick and Isabel smile at each other, making me nauseated.

"Alright, kids, you two enjoy your time together. I'll catch ya later."

I wave the two of them off, parting ways with the annoyingly happy couple. I think back on my relationship with Drew and on everything that's happened with Malcolm lately.

A couple of minutes later, I come to a conclusion in my mind. Drew's gotta go. I can't keep harboring feelings for Malcolm, not being able to do *anything* about them, not as long as Drew is still alive.

# Rick - Isabel's Apartment, June 2018

Isabel hands me a glass of ice-cold water on this hot and humid Saturday in June. I still can't believe she's mine. Although I also can't help but think back on all the times she's mentioned Drew's name since he's been missing. I think she has a *lot* of regrets about their relationship back in high school.

Isabel cuts my contemplation short.

"Hey, you wanna go to the park after lunch?"

I take a sip of my water.

"Sure, Izzy, but could you answer this one question for me please?"

Isabel sits down on the chair next to me.

"What's up?"

I slouch forward in my seat with my hands together, then turn my head to look at Isabel.

"Do you still have feelings for Drew?"

Isabel scrunches up her nose and eyes, shaking her head as if my question isn't valid.

"What?! What makes you think *that*? Drew and I haven't dated since high school. Plus, he's missing, and he's a drug addict. Drew and I would *never* work if they ever even find him. Also, I'm with *you*, dummy."

I sit back up in my seat and reach for Izzy's hand.

"That's great to hear, Iz, but did you *really* have to give me all those reasons?"

I retract my hand from Isabel's.

"You could've just said no. But instead, you made it *very* clear that you've been thinking about Drew a *lot* lately."

Isabel gets up and motions with her arms as she argues with me.

"What's wrong with *that*?! Am I not allowed to think about our friend from *middle school*? Drew is still *missing*, Rick! And all you can do is accuse me of having feelings for him?! How jealous do you have to be? The guy is literally nowhere near being a threat to our relationship, but you still make him out to be one!"

Isabel stomps into her kitchen. I definitely shouldn't have said anything.

I get up to follow her.

"Izzy, come on."

I reach for her arm after she fills a pitcher of ice with freshly steeped tea.

"I'm sorry, *okay*? I was acting like an idiot. I just care about you so much, you know? I can't help but believe Drew is alive and that he would sweep you right off your feet, just like he did in high school, as soon as he gets back into town."

Izzy turns towards me.

"Rick, you can't be jealous of a guy that is *clearly* not a threat to you. You have to be more confident in our relationship if you wanna move forward with me. Promise you'll stop being a jealous moron?"

I smirk, rolling my eyes at Isabel.

"Yeah, I *promise*, Izzy."

Isabel and I kiss to formally make up before we make our sandwiches.

I'm feeling more sure of my relationship with Isabel than ever before. The one thing that still bothers me, though, is how quickly Isabel dismissed Drew being a threat. Does she know something I don't? Could Drew Abston be dead, perhaps? Ah, I'm probably just paranoid. I'll let it go for the sake of our relationship. I wouldn't wanna accuse Izzy of withholding information from me after we just made up. I'll ask her when the time is right.

# Detective Paisley - The Abston House, July 2018

I take another sip of my fresh cup of coffee before I ask the Abstons my first question. The coffee is a *lot* better here than it is down at the station.

"Rebecca, could you tell me why you were in touch with the trailer kids downtown about finding and *beating* your son back in February?"

Roger looks at his wife in utter shock and disgust, releasing his hand from the back of her chair.

"*Rebecca*? How could you?!"

Rebecca tries her best to look over at her husband, shame seeping from her face as she bites her bottom lip.

"I'm *sorry*, Roger. Gene and I—"

Roger doesn't seem surprised or all too happy about any "Gene and Rebecca plotting."

"Gene and *you*?! Is that what you two talk about when you're over at his house? You could've fooled me! My *wife* and an elderly widowed man who lives next door to us, scheming up a plan to *rough up* our son?! I can't even *look* at you right now, Rebecca!"

Roger turns away, now gazing at the wall. I feel as though my role here is nothing more than the opposite of a marriage counselor. All I know is I *have* to figure out the reason why Drew is missing, then I can try to find him.

"I apologize. I didn't mean to cause any trouble, Mr. and Mrs. Abston. I'm merely trying to get to the bottom of this case. Now, if you could *please* answer my question, Rebecca."

Rebecca looks up at me with guilt-stricken eyes.

"Our son was missing for *two months*, detective. I had to do *something*!"

I'm starting to get impatient.

"It's a yes or no question, Mrs. Abston. Did you, or did you *not* send a hit out on your son?!"

Rebecca gets up, beginning to cry.

"YES! I DID, *OKAY?!*"

She takes a deep breath before continuing.

"I hired a group of three teenagers at the trailer park to find and beat Drew to teach him a lesson! He had been treating his family and friends with disrespect for *far* too long, and he was never going to change if something bad didn't happen to him! I know I'm a terrible mother, but at least I *care* about my son! I want, or *wanted* him to get better, OKAY?! Who knows if he's even still ALIVE!"

Rebecca sobs.

Roger walks over to his wife to console her.

"Rebecca, could you *please* calm down? It's not your fault he's missing. He got himself into this mess. But we have to be a united front; you can't keep things like this from me. And we have to be honest with Detective Paisley if we want any chance at finding our son, *okay*?"

Roger stretches his arms out to embrace Rebecca.

I think it's time for me to leave now that I've got my confession from Rebecca Abston. Not that I can incriminate her for it *now*, but at least I have a motive to build my case.

"Alright, I'm gonna get going now. Roger, Rebecca, it was nice to see you both. Thank you for being honest with me; it will only help with our efforts to find Drew. Have a good night."

I walk out of the Abston home, having become slightly more aware of the reason why Drew is missing.

# Roger - Frederick's Supermarket, October 2018

I've gotta get the essentials and get out. I can't have people looking at me and feeling sorry for my family and me for much longer. This is starting to become *too* much—we may have to move again. I reach down for peanut butter on the bottom shelf, then notice someone standing next to me. Not this again.

"Hello, Mr. Abston. How are you, Rebecca, and Anna holding up since Drew's death?"

It's Detective Robert Paisley; odd that he's here.

"Oh, hi, detective. I didn't realize you shopped here. We're doing alright; just hanging in."

I place the peanut butter in my cart and start to walk away.

"I'm sorry, I can't talk for long, detective. I have to get back home to make dinner for my family."

Detective Paisley doesn't say a *word* as I walk away. He just stands there in the middle of the peanut butter and jelly aisle as I walk towards the bread on the other end. I look back and notice him staring back at me; this is getting creepy.

I finish my shopping trip without seeing Robert again, then walk out into the parking lot, pushing my full cart towards my car. All of a sudden, I see Robert standing next to my minivan.

"Is there something I could *help* you with, detective?"

Robert Paisley puts on a fake smile.

"You tell *me*, Roger. Is there anything you're keeping from me about your son, Drew? Perhaps who might have killed him?"

I start quickly loading the food into my car. I don't appreciate the way the detective is treating me after I just lost my son.

"*NO*, detective! I don't know who killed my son! Now, if you'll *excuse* me, I have to get home."

I speedily drive out of the parking lot, far away from the stalker detective. I'll be telling the chief *all* about this riveting encounter I just had with one of his officers right after I tell my wife.

# Detective Paisley - Reggie's Diner, October 2018

I'm not wasting any more time. It's been *two months* since Drew Abston was murdered; I have to find the killer or killers behind this brutal crime.

I've been tailing Lisa Yantz all afternoon. She picked Malcolm Savona up from his trailer at three o' seven, and now she and he are sitting down for a late lunch at Reggie's Diner at three twenty-five.

I walk into the diner, right up to Malcolm and Lisa's table, prepared to question anything and everything.

"Hello, Mr. Savona. Hi there, Ms. Yantz. Would you two mind if I asked you some questions?"

Malcolm squirms in his seat, clearly feeling uncomfortable, while Lisa displays an extensive, disingenuous smile. She motions her hand towards the empty spot at their table.

"*Hi*, detective. No, not at all. Please, have a seat."

I pull a chair up to their table and sit down.

"Thank you. As you both know, I'm still searching for Drew Abston's killer. His body was found in that field up in Connecticut about a week after he died. An old farmer up there discovered him while riding his tractor. Now, I know you were both close with Drew, so tell me, why is it that you're able to sit here and have a laugh together while your friend's *murder* case still hasn't been solved? Could you explain that?"

Malcolm is the first to defend Lisa.

"Well, detective, we're just trying to move on. There isn't anything we can do to bring Drew back. Of *course* we're upset, but we've made our peace with his death. Now, if you'll excuse us."

Malcolm turns away from me, fixing his gaze back on Lisa. I'm not about to give up a fight.

"That's fine. I understand you two have grieved in your own way and have now made your peace with Drew's death. By the way, aren't you two *dating* as of last month?"

Lisa now stands up for herself and Malcolm.

"Yes, detective. Malcolm and I have been officially dating as of September. Is that a *crime*?"

I sit up straight.

"No, Lisa. It's not a *crime* to be in a relationship with someone. But tell me this, isn't it suspicious timing, being only a *month* after your so-called friend was killed? And you and Drew used to date, of course."

I turn towards Malcolm.

"How do you *live* with yourself, Malcolm? Knowing that you stole Lisa from your *best friend*? Your *dead* best friend, to make matters WORSE!"

Malcolm slams his hand down on the table, rattling everything on it, and stands up. This is the type of reaction I had hoped for.

"THAT'S *IT*! You're out of line, Detective Paisley! We answered *all* of your questions in the interrogation room last month, and now, you've overstayed your welcome. We don't have anything else to *say* to you! LEAVE US *ALONE*!"

I get up off my chair, surrendering my hands in the air.

"*Alright*, alright. I've heard all I needed to hear from you two. Especially *you*, Mr. Savona. I might be seeing you again *real* soon. Enjoy your lunch."

As I'm walking away, I know I earned another small victory in this case. Seeing the way Malcolm reacted to my simple line of questioning *truly* hit a nerve, and I'm going to find out why.

# Anna - Outside of Isabel's Apartment, October 2018

I am currently knocking on Isabel's apartment door on Saturday, October thirteenth, at twelve thirty-six in the afternoon. After about thirty knocks, Isabel begrudgingly answers the door.

"*What is it*?! Oh, it's you, Anna. Well, come on in, I suppose."

I roll my eyes at Isabel's lack of hospitality.

"It's nice to see you too, Isabel."

Isabel stands behind the counter in her kitchen, offering me a seat on one of the stools in front of her.

"What can I help you with, Anna?"

I sit down on Isabel's uncomfortably stiff kitchen stool.

"I was wondering if you had any answers to Drew's death. Is there *anything* you could tell me? I'm just trying to find closure for myself and my family. God knows that detective hasn't been of any help."

Isabel folds her hands together on top of the kitchen counter.

"I don't know what you want me to say, Anna. Rick and I offered to help Drew the day before he disappeared. We went to his trailer the next morning, and he was already gone."

This isn't going anywhere; I'm going to have to bring up the past.

"Yeah, but you and Drew dated for like a week back in high school, right?"

Isabel twitches her nose.

"Yeah, so?"

I cross my legs, leaning forward in my seat.

"And wasn't Rick jealous of the whole thing? Oh, and then, of course, the *fabulous* Lisa Yantz stepped into the picture and stole him from you, right?"

Isabel is getting flustered, I can tell.

"*Where* are you going with this, Anna?"

A devious smile develops on my face.

"Hear me out, Iz. What if Rick, after *all* these years later, got revenge on his old friend Drew for stealing you from him back in high school and *killed* Drew?"

Isabel is completely taken aback.

"ANNA! You can't just *say* stuff like that! Rick would *never* harm anyone, *especially* not Drew. He and Drew were close in high school, and I know he still cares about him."

I'm prepared to stand down, at least on that particular topic.

"*Okay*, Iz. I understand. How about *you*, then? Would you've wanted revenge for the way Drew treated you back in high school? *Dumping* you for Lisa?"

Isabel crosses her arms.

"What are you trying to *say*, Anna?"

I twirl my hair to the side.

"I'm just trying to find out who may have killed my brother, Isabel; that's all. So, did you *kill* him or not?"

Isabel rushes over to me, picking me up off my chair and forcefully walking me over to the door. I *completely* underestimated this tiny girl's strength.

"You gotta *go*, Anna! *NO*, I DIDN'T KILL YOUR BROTHER! I *LOVED* HIM! AND THEN HE CHOSE LISA, AND THEN HIGH SCHOOL WAS *OVER*!"

Isabel breaks down into tears on the wooden floor of her apartment.

"What else do you want me to *say*, Anna?! I still love Drew to this day, and now he's *GONE*! I'm so grateful for Rick, but Drew was my first love, and we never even got a real chance to be together! I should've reached out to him sooner before his life went down in smoke so suddenly. That will be the biggest regret of my life."

Isabel abruptly stands back up, pushing me towards the exit.

"Now, *PLEASE* LEAVE! I can't be reminded of him anymore."

I pat Isabel on the shoulder as I'm standing outside of her apartment.

"I'm *so* sorry, Isabel. I didn't know you cared that much about Drew. He didn't deserve you, just know that. Rick is the best thing that's ever happened to you; don't mess that up."

Isabel sucks up her tears as she starts shutting her door.

"Just *leave*, Anna!"

Alright, either that was *really* good acting, or Isabel really *isn't* a suspect in Drew's murder. Only time will tell.

# Detective Paisley - Anna's Office, October 2018

I have to go interrogate the sister one last time. This time, I'm approaching her at her personal office. It's time to get to the bottom of this murder case, and catching people off guard is a surefire way to do that.

I knock on the front door of Anna's office. About ten seconds later, she opens up the door.

"Detective Paisley? What are *you* doing here?"

"Hi, Anna. Is it okay if I come in? I have a few questions for you regarding Drew's death."

Anna opens the door fully, welcoming me in.

"Sure, detective. Come on in."

I make myself at home and sit down by the small table in her office. Anna sits down across from me.

"What would you like to know, detective?"

I take out my memo pad and flip up to a new page.

"My team noticed an outgoing call on Drew's phone at one-thirty four in the morning from New Hampshire the night of July seventeenth, two thousand and eighteen. That call was to *you*, Ms. Abston. Care to explain what that call was about?"

Anna seems defeated. She just wants to know what happened to her brother.

"Yeah, so that call was Drew *finally* getting in touch with me after *months* of not seeing him or knowing where he was."

I jot down a few notes.

"But of course, you two were in touch via secret letters through which you used pseudonyms, correct?"

Anna nods her head.

"Correct. My name was Suzanne Wilkerson, and Drew's name was Jimmy Morris. I wrote every letter in pen while Drew used a pencil. Maybe he thought his words would be less permanent that way, I don't know."

I write down a few more notes.

"Okay, Anna. Tell me what you and Drew talked about on the phone that night."

Anna sits up straight, preparing me for a story.

"That night, Drew called me out of *nowhere*, and I was so relieved to hear from him...."

Drew gets out of bed from his attic bedroom, silently stepping into Curtis and Samantha's room. Inching quietly towards Curtis' nightstand, he reaches into the top drawer, discovering his cell phone is just lying there next to Curtis'.

Drew walks back to his room, then powers his phone on and gleefully watches as the lights bring it back to life. Quickly, Drew goes to the favorites on his contacts list, tapping on Anna's name to call her. A few rings later, Anna picks up.

"*Drew*?! Is that you?!"

Drew whispers back to Anna.

"Anna! I have to be quiet, or else my landlords will wake up. I'm not supposed to be using my phone."

Anna sits up in her bed.

"Well of *course* you're not supposed to be using your phone, you dummy! Don't you realize someone could track your phone and *find you*?!"

Drew creaks a step closer to his bed, taking a seat.

"I know, I know. This is probably the dumbest thing I've ever done; I just had to talk to you. Remember when we were kids, Anna? And we used to be best friends?"

Anna looks around her room, searching for memories of Drew in her mind.

"Yeah, those were the good ole days, Drew. But then you got into fights, and I would stick up for you and get in trouble too."

Drew fiddles with the vintage porcelain trinket box on his dresser.

"Yeah, but you didn't *really* get in trouble, Anna. The principal just reprimanded you for getting involved in my problems; he never *actuall*y punished you."

Anna rolls her eyes.

"Yeah, well, it was just as bad. And anyway, Drew, it's been *years* since we were kids. You've gotten yourself into a *lot* more trouble since then. When are you gonna come home and fix the mess you made?"

Drew gets up again, pacing in his room.

"I almost have enough to pay the cartel back in a couple of months. I owe them a *lot* of money, Anna."

Anna gets up out of bed, walking over to her moonlit window.

"How *much* money, Drew?!"

Drew stands by the small window in his attic apartment, staring up at the full moon.

"About twelve hundred. And I would've paid it back sooner, but Curtis and Samantha only give me fifty bucks a week to work on their farm, which didn't start until sometime in March. And *trust* me, they're being generous because they don't have much to give. And it's not like I have any other options, being wanted by the cartel and all."

Anna sits down, overwhelmed by Drew's debt.

"How do you owe them *that* much, Drew?! Isn't heroin dirt cheap?!"

Drew combs his fingers through his overgrown, chestnut hair.

"Yeah, but I asked them for a loan once back in November because I wanted to start up that music store I was telling you about. I needed a down payment for the lease on a storefront downtown. Remember where Yellow Umbrella Shake Shack used to be?"

Anna bites her fingernails, a nervous habit.

"Yeah, I remember it well. They had the *best* shakes. When we were kids, I used to get—wait, *why* would you ever borrow money from the *cartel*, Drew?!"

Drew launches himself back-first onto his thin, bumpy mattress.

"I don't know, Anna. Probably because no bank in town would ever trust a *drug* dealer like me anymore. I had to get out of dealing. I knew that. And I had to get clean, but I didn't know how to; it was too hard."

Anna throws her phone down onto her bed, roughly running her fingers through her hair in distress. She takes a deep breath. Meanwhile, Drew is panicking through the phone at a faint volume.

"Anna? *Anna*?! You there?!"

Anna unenthusiastically picks her phone back up.

"*Yeah*, I'm here, Drew."

Drew calms himself back down.

"*Anyway*, as I was saying, I used the money to make a down payment on the storefront. And then Lisa and I broke up, and I sunk deeper into my addiction. Having no money to pay back the cartel or to make the first monthly payment on rent for the store, I fled. And it wasn't just the adult responsibility that scared me off. It was the fact that my *life* was in danger. And now I can finally breathe again, Anna.

I'm ready to come back in September to pay off my debts and start over in Woodbank."

Anna feels a sense of relief for her older brother's sake.

"Alright, well, stay safe and keep working hard, bro. I'm proud of you, Drew, for getting clean and getting your life on the right track. I hope to see you in September. Love you, Jimmy."

Drew laughs.

"Love you, Suzanne. I'll be seeing you *real* soon."

"And that's the last I ever heard from my brother. No more phone calls, no more letters."

Anna starts to cry.

"I never got to say *goodbye*, let alone see him sober again, detective. Do you know how that *feels*?!"

I decide to console Anna rather than push her any further. The poor girl has been through enough.

"No. I don't, Anna, and I'm so sorry for your loss. Truly, I am. I'm doing everything I can to find out who killed Drew."

Anna suddenly gets up. I can sense an outburst brewing within her.

"I don't think that you *are* doing everything you can, detective! Otherwise, you would've found Drew's killer by now! NOW GET *OUT*!"

Anna points with her whole right arm towards the door. It's my queue to leave.

"Okay, Ms. Abston. I'm sorry for upsetting you. Thank you for your time."

Anna slams the door shut on me as soon as I walk out of her office.

I've got my work cut out for me.

# Drew - The Farm, July 2018

Without any warning, I'm awoken to the sound of someone slamming a ladder onto the window of my attic room at two thirty-eight in the morning. Sitting straight up in bed, I decide to be brave and confront the intruder.

"WHO'S THERE?!"

The beam of a flashlight pours into my room, blinding my vision.

With great force, a man shatters my window, entering my room with his loud, heavy boots on the ground. I have no idea who this could be; he has a mask on to conceal his identity. I'm so petrified that my voice cracks; I don't think I've ever been this afraid in my life.

"*WHO ARE YOU*?!"

The unresponsive man grabs both of my arms, yanking me out of bed, then zip ties my hands together.

"*HELP*!"

Before I can yell again, the man quickly pulls out a roll of duct tape, rips a piece off, and sticks it over my mouth. He then pulls me towards the door to my room.

The strong man drags me all the way outside, through the front door, all while holding a 9mm pistol in his free hand. As I am being dragged out of the house, Curtis and Samantha are sound asleep in their bedroom.

When we get to the man's car, he shoves me in the trunk, then starts speeding out of the driveway. Over the course of an hours-long drive (I'm guessing it was over three hours), my mind races.

As I'm trying to figure out who this man is that just *abducted* me, I think back on all the people that are mad at me. My parents, for one, but would they really *abduct* me?! I don't know if they have it in them. Then, of course, there's my little sister Anna; but *why* would she do this to me? We just spoke on the phone last night, and we ended our conversation on good terms. And then there's *Malcolm*. That guy has secretly resented me ever since I stole Lisa from him back in high school.

All at once, the car comes to a halt. The man opens up the trunk, pulls me out, and starts walking me over to a secluded warehouse. We are *literally* in the middle of nowhere because the perimeter of the building is surrounded by farmland. From the sight of dawn, I sense it's around six in the morning.

The man opens up the door to this abandoned warehouse, cuts my zip tie, and shoves me to the floor. He then leaves, locking the door behind him. I'm left lying on the ground in utter seclusion, still hoping I can somehow make it home to Woodbank alive.

# Drew - The Warehouse, August 2018

Two and a half weeks later, someone finally enters the warehouse. I've been surviving off a pallet of crackers and water bottles I found in a corner of the tightly locked building. Whoever set this space up for me was even kind enough to leave a few buckets to serve as toilets; how nice of them.

A man appears in the warehouse around midnight, wearing the same black balaclava mask as before. He's holding a lantern in his left hand as he approaches me. All of a sudden, he rips the mask off.

To no surprise, I've never seen him in my life. The man has wavy, dark brown hair with thick eyebrows and a large, pointed nose. There are wrinkles all over his face, so I'm guessing he's in his late fifties. The man is wearing a gray plaid shirt with beat-up jeans and black work boots.

The man speaks to me with a sadistic tone.

"*Hello*, Drew. I've come to see how you've been doing. Has your stay with us been *exceptional*? HA HA!"

His hyena laugh makes my skin crawl.

"Before you ask me any questions, Drew, I'm going to be asking *you* a few."

The man sits down on an unused, overturned bucket.

"Now, how long have you been dealing heroin?"

I can't even stand up straight, let alone try to attack this guy because I'm so weak from malnutrition. Plus, he's aiming his 9mm right at me. His handgun is casually resting on his right thigh as he grips it with his right hand.

"I don't know. I started in July of twenty-seventeen, I think. Then I stopped sometime in early December. So for about five months, I dealt heroin; I *don't* anymore."

The man leans slightly forward in his seat.

"Well, good for *you*, Andrew. Next question. How long did you and *Isabel Tabbert* go out?"

I'm thinking back on my one-week relationship with Izzy back in high school, scrambling for the importance of this question.

"What?! Why does *that* matter?!"

The man slams his left boot down on the ground as hard as he can.

"JUST *ANSWER* THE QUESTION!"

I curl up in a ball against the concrete wall behind me in self-defense.

"Okay, *OKAY*! Izzy and I went out for one week, and then I dumped her for Lisa. I *know* it was selfish. I loved Isabel, but then came Lisa, and I knew I had to give it a shot."

The man is dissatisfied with my answer.

"Alright, that was a good enough answer, I *suppose*. Next question. What in the *world* made you think it was okay to steal Isabel from your best friend Rick in the first place?!"

This questionnaire is starting to become *very* strange. How does this man that I've never met know so much about me?

"To be honest, Rick and I had a subtle understanding that we both liked Isabel. We both talked about her *all* the time when she wasn't around. And then, one day, I decided to do something about it. I truly never thought the guy would *ever* do anything about his feelings for Iz. Looking back now, I know I was self-centered and overly confident. I should apologize to both of them when I get back into town."

The man lights a cigarette.

"What makes you think you're getting back to town? You haven't passed the test yet. Besides, don't you think it's a little *late* for apologies, Mr. Abston? You've hurt *so many people.*"

My body jolts upwards into a standing position. I'm now ready to stand up for myself.

"And what makes you think you can judge *me*?!"

The man walks right up to me and pushes the barrel of his pistol against my forehead.

"Watch who you're talking to; *I'm* the one holding the gun."

The man sits back down, preparing for his next question, I assume.

"And how about Malcolm Savona. Why would you ever think it was okay to stab your business partner in the back, Drew?!"

I sit back down on the cracked, concrete floor that is covered in dirt.

"I wasn't thinking clearly; all I wanted to do was get high. I don't know what else to tell you, sir. And to save you some time, it was the same with my dad, my mom, and my sister Anna. I just wanted the fix, and I put that above everything and everyone. You become selfish when you're an addict. And even before I became an addict, I was a self-absorbed person."

The man inhales his cigarette for three seconds, then lets out a plume of smoke in my direction.

"Very well, Mr. Abston. You've been paying for your sins long enough. But before you can pass the test, you need to explain to me your relationship with Lisa Yantz."

I look up at the man in front of me, more puzzled now than ever.

"*What*? What do you want me to say about Lisa? I wanted to marry her, and I told her that. And then she saw me go through my addiction and make bad choices and decided to *dump* me for Malcolm. What else is there to say about Lisa? I still love her, and I always will, but I don't know if I'll ever get over what she did."

The man looks at me, squinting his eyes to show his full curiosity.

"And what exactly did she *do* to you, Drew? All she ever did was love you, and you pushed her away. Of course she dumped you for your best friend. She was *sick* of you, Drew! And so was everyone else in your life! Of *course* you ended up in a locked warehouse, only to be tortured by silence and darkness without proper hygiene or food for over TWO WEEKS!"

The man springs up and lunges towards me.

"AND NOW YOU'RE GOING TO PAY!"

The man presses his 9mm into the left side of my skull, ready to shoot and kill me, until someone interrupts him. Another man walks into the warehouse. *This* man I recognize.

"*DAD*?! Is that *you*?!"

I start speed walking towards my father, overjoyed that he has come to my rescue. The two men that are walking into the warehouse with him are holding rifles, blocking me from approaching my dad.

With two rifles pointed straight at me, I back off with my hands lifted high.

"*Dad*? What's going on?"

My dad pushes through the two men, walking up to me.

"It's okay, fellas. This is my son, Drew."

My dad reaches in to hug me tightly, then releases his arms a few seconds later.

"Drew, do you know why you're here?"

I'm confused as to why *he's* here as well.

"I have *no* idea. I was kidnapped from a house I was staying at in New Hampshire and brought here by *this* guy."

I point my weak, shaky arm towards the man with the lantern.

"Who *is* he, dad? And why are *you* here? Are these guys holding you hostage because of me?"

My father closes his eyes, shaking his head as he starts to laugh.

"No, no, no, Drew. I'm not being held hostage by anybody. Do you have any *idea* who I *am*?"

I look at my dad with eyes of bewilderment. Frightened by the man who spawned me, I slowly step backward away from him. I've never been this afraid of Roger Abston in my life.

"I guess not... who exactly *are* you, dad?"

My dad starts pacing around the warehouse, tapping his fingers together.

"Have I ever told you about my father, Drew?"

I glance around the warehouse, trying to remember Grandpa Joe. A smile grows on my face as pleasant memories wash over me.

"Grandpa *Joe*? Oh yeah! He was the best grandpa—*way* better than mom's dad."

My dad laughs.

"Oh, of *course*. He was *far* better than Grandpa Steve. That man was so grumpy, and he wanted *everybody* to know it."

I chuckle as I remember my crusty old grandfather.

"Yeah, Grandpa Steve was *such* a grouch. Grandpa *Joe*, on the other hand, used to give Anna and me gifts every time he came over to the house. He was the greatest. I wish he was still alive."

My dad's blissful grin prematurely transforms into a look of pure hatred.

"Yeah, *well*, I don't. And do you wanna know *why*, Drew? Because he *RUINED* MY LIFE! Just look where you are, Andrew. *LOOK AROUND YOU*! Is *this* the legacy of a *good* guy? I DON'T THINK SO! You wanna *really* know why I'm here, Drew? Because *I'm* your boss—or former boss. And you still owe me money. Of course, I'm not talking about the two hundred and fifty dollars you stole from my landscaping business; you already paid me back for that. I'm talking about the loan you took from me to start up your little music store in town."

I begin to feel dizzy as sheer confusion and shock flood my mind.

"*WHAT*?! That loan wasn't from *you*. It was from the cartel."

My dad bursts out with a cackle that's about twenty seconds too long. After his eruption of laughter, he finally speaks.

"*Son*, I *am* the cartel."

My head starts spinning in circles, my eyes following suit.

"*What* are you *talking* about, *dad*?!"

My eyes dart towards the three men who are holding guns.

"Are they forcing you to say these things?!"

My dad calmly walks toward me.

"*No*, son. Nobody is forcing me to do anything. BUT YOU ARE FORCING ME TO DO *THIS*!"

I quickly put both of my arms up, crisscrossed in front of my face in self-defense. After I notice I'm not in any danger, I look up at my father again.

"Forcing you to do *what* exactly?!"

Tears start streaming from my father's eyes.

"*Andrew*... the male bloodline in our family has *got* to come to an end. We're no good."

My dad starts pacing again.

"Are you prepared to pay for the sins you've committed against your friends, your family, and *me*?"

I start to slowly walk backward again, away from my father.

"And what exactly is the *cost*, dad?"

My dad sprints up to me and quick-draws his pistol, aiming it right against my forehead.

"IT'S *THIS*!"

*BANG*!

My body takes a two-part fall, knees folding to the ground first. Then my torso slides down to the right, onto the cold, hard concrete surface. My bleeding head rattles against the floor as the four men watch my earthly life disappear, not one of them flinching.

I watch from above as my soul seeps slowly out of the shell that was once Andrew Roger Abston.

# Detective Paisley - The Abston House, August 2018

Deep regrets are weighing on my chest as I approach the Abston house. Before I can even knock, Rebecca Abston opens up the front door.

"Detective *Paisley*? What brings you by? Do you have any news about Drew?!"

I take a deep breath, then sigh.

"Mrs. Abston, your son is dead."

Rebecca collapses onto the foyer floor, then starts to wail so sorrowfully—unlike anything I've ever heard.

"I'm sorry, Rebecca. Please accept my condolences."

Roger Abston walks over, starting to cry after hearing the news.

"Our—our boy is *DEAD*?! No, no, no... it can't be. You must be mistaken, detective."

I reach out my hand to console Roger on his shoulder.

"I'm sorry, Mr. Abston... Drew is dead. He was found lying out in a field down in Connecticut early this morning. A farmer found him while he was out on his tractor; he was on his way to harvest corn crops."

Roger Abston picks his wife up off the floor, holding her tightly.

"Let's go sit down in the living room, Rebecca. Detective, thank you. You've done enough. Please let us know who did this to our boy. *Please*, as soon as you know."

I put my hands behind my back and stand up straight.

"Rest assured you will be the *first* to know, I promise."

# Roger - The Abston House, October 2018

As I lay here in bed, I twist and turn, sweaty and in a panic. These past two months have been filled with questions upon questions from Detective Paisley. All he knows is that Drew was killed over a week before he was found by that farmer up in Connecticut.

Robert Paisley is *relentless*; he won't stop until he finds out who murdered Drew.

I cannot *believe* I killed my own son. Part of me feels like I can tough out the rest of my life knowing I did it, and the other part of me can't bear another moment of this guilt.

I thought I did the right thing, ending the direct male Abston bloodline, from which no good has come. Now I can see why my father died a miserable death in that hospital bed, rotting from the inside out from Hodgkin's lymphoma. I deserve the same fate.

I lay here restless, next to my wife, Rebecca, who doesn't have the *slightest* clue that I'm the leader of the cartel.

Not being able to take one more minute of this immeasurable shame, I grab my robe and head to the garage. As I'm pulling out with my car, I start calling Detective Paisley. Surprisingly, he answers only one ring later, at eleven thirty at night. It's almost as if he's been waiting for my phone call all night.

"*Hello*? Roger Abston? Is everything alright?"

Sweat starts to bead up on my forehead as my heart pounds. I need to release this feeling that's been choking me for months.

"No, Detective Paisley, everything is *not* alright! I, I... I killed my own son!"

I immediately slam the brakes and put my car into park in the middle of the road, dropping my phone on my lap and sobbing face down into my palms.

I can hear the detective shouting at me through the phone at a dull volume.

"ROGER! *ROGER*?! ARE YOU THERE?!"

A few seconds later, I pick the phone back up, bringing it up to my ear.

"*Yes*, I'm here."

The detective is panicking again.

"Are you telling me that you *killed* your son, Drew Abston?!"

I look up at the full moon, finally being able to breathe again.

"Yes... I shot my own son. I thought I needed to take care of him—to end his suffering, the same suffering I've endured for over *twenty* years. I took over my father's business as soon as he died. I'm a *drug dealer*, detective. And even worse, I'm the head of it all. I need to get out of this... even if it means losing everything. I'm ready."

Detective Paisley doesn't utter a single word for about five seconds. At long last, he responds to my confession.

"Okay, Roger—stay where you are. I'm coming to find you. This can all end now; you don't have to cause your family any more pain."

Eight minutes later, Robert Paisley is pulling up to my car, which is a block away from my house. He gets out of his car, then pulls me out of mine, handcuffing me in the middle of Rose Street. After he reads me my rights, we journey to Woodbank Precinct.

Detective Paisley brings me up to the interrogation room, where I was once an innocent man. This time, the visit isn't as friendly.

"Now, Roger, tell me how you found your son."

I start to fiddle with my thumbs now that I have limited dexterity.

"I have a guy who hacks phones. We noticed a ping on Drew's phone when he called my daughter, Anna. It wasn't difficult to find him after that. I sent a guy up to that farm in New Hampshire to take Drew to my warehouse in Connecticut. I wanted him to suffer there, thinking about all the things he'd done to the people in his life; all of the *pain* he caused them."

Detective Paisley inquires further.

"I see... Roger, answer me this final question. Why did you leave your son's dead body out in the middle of a *corn*field in Connecticut?"

Repositioning myself in my seat, I carefully arrange in my mind a sufficient explanation for the detective.

"Detective... I left Drew's cold, dead body all alone down there in that field simply because I couldn't bring him home. You see, how would it look to you and my family if I just so happened to have discovered Drew's body? I couldn't risk being outed on anyone's terms but my own."

Detective Paisley peers into my soul with an emotionless face.

"Very well then, Roger... Thank you for—*clarifying* that."

The breath of remorse vacates my lungs towards the detective.

"Looking back at it now... I realize *I* was the true villain all along, as was my father. Drew was just trying to get his life back and make a difference in the world. I stole that from him, and I know there's no taking that back..."

Tears start to flow from my eyes.

"I'm the *real* monster of Woodbank, Massachusetts. And I don't expect any sympathy—not even from my wife or daughter... I can live with that punishment."

Robert Paisley sits up in his chair, leaning towards me with interlocked hands.

"Well, you better be prepared to live with that, Roger, for the rest of your sad, miserable years on earth. You took away an innocent man's life, your *own son's* life. You oughta be ashamed of yourself."

I lower my head onto my hands, not being able to look the detective in the eye any longer.

"Oh, *I am*, Robert. I am."

Somehow, I acquire enough courage to look back up at the detective.

"I murdered my own son on August fourth, with one bullet to the head. I'll never forget that day. Never, ever, EVER, *EVER*!"

With each "ever," I slam my head down onto the table. I deserve torment, so I'm going to give it to myself. The detective even lets me do it, smiling as his case has come to a close.

# Anna - In her office, October 2018

As we prepare for the funeral of my older brother, Andrew Roger Abston, I can't help but have a deep-seated hatred for our father. Roger Abston took away the life of someone who was about to start over. Drew wanted a second chance, a fresh start; our father took that away from him.

It's been two days since my dad confessed to Detective Paisley that he killed his only son. Ever since then, I've been working on the eulogy for Drew's funeral, now that my mom and I have closure at last.

Andrew Abston was a musical genius. He played the guitar, drums, banjo, harmonica, and saxophone like a pro. He hadn't played for about a year—not since he got into dealing and using drugs. Drew wasn't easy to have as a brother, but he was my best friend for as long as I can remember.

Drew got into fights, but he also brought people together. He was always there for you when you needed him the most. Sometimes he would disappear for seemingly no reason at all, but that was just one of his faults. Drew struggled with rage and bipolar disorder. One day he was up, doing a million things at once, and the next day, he would be lying on the couch, flipping through the TV channels as he hid from the world.

I think Drew's way of handling his stress and anxiety was picking fights. I can't describe it any other way. And although he may have seemed scary at times, he was the most loving person I ever knew. Drew never gave up on me or anyone else he loved. He was a great brother, son, friend, and boyfriend to whoever was crazy enough to date him. Anyone who knew Drew was richly blessed. You just wanted him in your life forever as soon as you met him.

Sadly, drugs took over Drew's life, and it crushed me, my parents, and all of his loved ones. Eventually, he chose the high before anything else. With that said, Drew made the choice to get his life back on track. He decided he wanted to become a selfless person and start focusing on the people he loved rather than himself.

Drew's last letter to me before he died talked about how he was ready to come back to Woodbank and make amends with everyone now that he was clean. He told me he almost had enough money to pay the cartel back for the drugs he stole and for the loan he took out from them. Drew wanted to start his music store as soon as he was back in town. He wanted to teach people his craft. He wanted to make people smile.

My mom, Rebecca, and I, alongside Rick Malloy and Isabel Tabbert, are going to make sure Drew's business thrives in honor of him. Anyone who is musically talented, please speak with us; we would love to have you on our team of instructors and salesmen and women. The old Yellow Umbrella Shake Shack will now be called "Drew's Sound." And please, never forget my brother. When you walk past the music store or come in to visit, please remember Drew's legacy. He wanted to make people happy. He just didn't always know how to do it. And now I see him living on in that store forever, looking down on us and smiling as people find joy through music. Thank you.

# Anna - Reggie's Diner, October 2018

Now that Drew's funeral is over, everyone who was close to him is sitting with my mom and me having an early dinner at Reggie's. Suddenly, I receive a note across the table from Rick. He and Isabel secretly nod at me.

`You wanna know who hacked your brother's phone that night? Look to the left of Malcolm.`

I look over at the person sitting to the left of Malcolm, and there sits Lisa Yantz. I get up, furious.

"*Lisa*?! Did you hack Drew's phone the day he was kidnapped?!"

Lisa stands up, preparing to defend herself.

"*No*! Of course not, Anna! Who gave you a crazy idea like that?!"

I flail the note from Rick and Isabel around in the air.

"Well, you went to school for computer programming, *didn't you*?!"

Lisa gulps so loudly that everyone can hear it. She focuses her eyes in every direction but mine, guilt written all over her face.

"Yeah... *so*?"

Malcolm interjects, defending his lady as usual.

"Leave her *alone*, Anna! Why would you accuse Lisa of something like that?! Are you *that* desperate for answers that you're going to grasp for straws?! You're better than that, Anna, *really*."

Rick gets up.

"Isabel and I have been doing a bit of investigating behind the scenes, Anna. We found Lisa's college diploma that proves she got her bachelor's in computer programming. We also know she was on her computer early that morning after you and Drew spoke on the phone. Isabel snuck into Lisa's house one afternoon while Lisa was at work and looked at her browsing history. She had all sorts of hacking engines listed the morning of July seventeenth on her browser."

Lisa gives Isabel the death stare.

"*How did you get into my house, you SNAKE*?!"

Isabel stands up, crossing her arms.

"It was easy, really. I just snuck into your shed in the backyard, grabbed a ladder, and made my way up to your unlocked bedroom window."

Isabel scoffs at Lisa.

"*Stupid* easy, if you ask me."

Lisa leaps over the food-filled table, knocking over wine glasses and smooshing every plate until scraps stain every inch of her white blouse.

"YOU'RE *DEAD*, ISABEL! YOU HEAR ME?!"

Lisa reaches in and grabs Isabel by the throat, strangling her with both hands against the restaurant wall.

Rick grabs Lisa's left arm.

"LET *GO* OF HER, LISA!"

Malcolm yanks Lisa's right arm.

"LISA! *SNAP OUT OF IT*!"

I step in and assist in removing Lisa's clutches from Isabel.

Finally, Lisa releases her grasp from Isabel's throat as we successfully pull her away. That woman has super strength when she's enraged.